D1166444

# THE COUNTRY WIFE

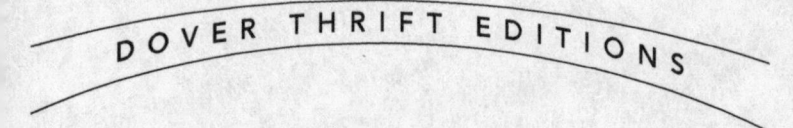

DOVER THRIFT EDITIONS

## William Wycherley

DOVER PUBLICATIONS, INC.
GARDEN CITY, NEW YORK

## DOVER THRIFT EDITIONS

GENERAL EDITOR: SUSAN L. RATTINER
EDITOR OF THIS VOLUME: GREGORY KOUTROUBY

*Bibliographical Note*

This Dover edition, first published in 2018, is an unabridged republication of a standard edition of the work, originally published in 1675.

*Library of Congress Cataloging-in-Publication Data*

Names: Wycherley, William, 1640–1716, author.
Title: The country wife / William Wycherley.
Description: Mineola, New York : Dover Publications, 2018. |
Series: Dover thrift editions
Identifiers: LCCN 2017036973| ISBN 9780486817538
    (paperback) | ISBN 0486817539 (paperback)
Subjects: LCSH: London (England)—Drama. | Married
    women—Drama. | Seduction—Drama. | BISAC: DRAMA /
    English, Irish, Scottish, Welsh. | GSAFD: Comedies.
Classification: LCC PR3774 .C6 2018 | DDC 822/.4—dc23
LC record available at https://lccn.loc.gov/2017036973

Manufactured in the United States by LSC Communications
81753902    2020
www.doverpublications.com

# Note

In 1660, THE Protectorate, the ruling power in England, gave way to the Restoration, during which Charles II was called back from his lengthy European exile and the monarchy was restored (Charles had departed England after Oliver Cromwell, the dictatorial Lord Protector, had defeated him in 1651, the close of the English Civil War). Amid tensions regarding the role of religion in English society and the governing power of Parliament, London was also exposed to the hardships of the Great Plague of 1665 and the Great Fire of London (1666).

Nevertheless, the latter part of the seventeenth century was an extremely fertile period for English literature. Fiction, journalism, and especially drama were flourishing. Charles II, an enthusiastic theatergoer, encouraged dramatic productions in London, leading to a proliferation of new plays, as well as the reopening of the theaters themselves after a ban instituted under the Puritans. To a great extent, the concerns of the plays reflected those of the court and the upper classes—Charles's social milieu and a key component of the theatergoing public.

The comedy of manners, as perfected by the preeminent French playwright Molière (1622–1673), was an important influence on the work of the Restoration dramatists. The English writers featured bawdy, risqué plot devices, witty dialogue, and double entendres in their comic treatment of the relations between the sexes and the behavior of society's upper crust. The artifice of courtly behavior provided many opportunities for amusing repartee as well.

A common element of numerous Restoration comedies was the rake—a stylish gentleman whose contempt for society's conventions lent themselves to farce and cruel game-playing. In *The Country Wife* by William Wycherley (ca. 1640–1716), a predatory rake, Harry Horner, seduces the wives of a number of gullible husbands.

His pursuits take an unexpected turn after his encounter with a supposedly ingenuous country wife, whose jealous, abusive husband proclaims, "If we do not cheat women, they'll cheat us." The notion that marriage is anything but sacrosanct among the privileged classes frequently is played upon—in fact, most of the characters in *The Country Wife* are willing participants in cheating and deceit of one sort or another.

Wycherley's comedy was first performed in 1675. Because its content and language were considered unacceptable for public display due to their suggestiveness, *The Country Wife* was not performed for many years; an expurgated version by David Garrick was substituted for the provocative original, which is enjoyed today for its wit and wisdom.

# Contents

# Dramatis Personae

MR. HORNER
MR. HARCOURT
MR. DORILANT
MR. PINCHWIFE
MR. SPARKISH
SIR JASPER FIDGET
MRS. MARGERY PINCHWIFE
MRS. ALITHEA
LADY FIDGET
MRS. DAINTY FIDGET
MRS. SQUEAMISH
OLD LADY SQUEAMISH
LUCY, *Alithea's Maid*
*A Boy*
*A Quack*
*Waiters, Servants, and Attendants*

SCENE—*London*

2

*Indignior quicquam reprehendi, non quia crassè*
*Compositum illepideve putetur, sed quia nuper:*
*Nec veniam Antiquis, sed honorem & præmia posci.*
                                        HORAT.[1]

# PROLOGUE

### Spoken by MR. HORNER

Poets, like cudgell'd bullies, never do
At first or second blow submit to you;
But will provoke you still, and ne'er have done,
Till you are weary first with laying on.
The late so baffled scribbler of this day,
Though he stands trembling, bids me boldly say,
What we before most plays are us'd to do,
For poets out of fear first draw on you;
In a fierce prologue the still pit defy,
And, ere you speak, like Castril give the lie.
But though our Bayes's battles oft I've fought,
And with bruis'd knuckles their dear conquests bought;
Nay, never yet fear'd odds upon the stage,
In prologue dare not hector with the age,
But would take quarter from your saving hands,
Though Bayes within all yielding countermands,
Says you confed'rate wits no quarter give,
Therefore his play shan't ask your leave to live.
Well, let the vain rash fop, by huffing so,
Think to obtain the better terms of you;
But we, the actors, humbly will submit,

---

[1] I hate to see something criticized not on the grounds that it is clumsy and inelegant, but simply because it is modern. I hate to see people demand not merely indulgence for the older writers, but the actual prerogative of idolatry.—Horace, *Epistles*, 1,1, 76–78.

Now, and at any time, to a full pit;
Nay, often we anticipate your rage,
And murder poets for you on our stage:
We set no guards upon our tiring-room,
But when with flying colours there you come,
We patiently, you see, give up to you
Our poets, virgins, nay, our matrons too.

# ACT I

*Enter* HORNER, *and* QUACK *following him at a distance*

HORN. [*aside*]    A quack is as fit for a pimp as a midwife for a bawd; they are still but in their way, both helpers of nature.—— [*aloud*] Well, my dear Doctor, hast thou done what I desired?

QUACK.    I have undone you for ever with the women, and reported you throughout the whole town as bad as an eunuch, with as much trouble as if I had made you one in earnest.

HORN.    But have you told all the midwives you know, the orange wenches at the playhouses, the city husbands, and old fumbling keepers of this end of the town, for they'll be the readiest to report it?

QUACK.    I have told all the chambermaids, waiting-women, tire-women, and old women of my acquaintance; nay, and whispered it as a secret to 'em, and to the whisperers of Whitehall; so that you need not doubt 'twill spread, and you will be as odious to the handsome young women as——

HORN.    As the small-pox. Well——

QUACK.    And to the married women of this end of the town, as——

HORN.    As the great ones; nay, as their own husbands.

QUACK.    And to the city dames, as aniseed Robin, of filthy and contemptible memory; and they will frighten their children with your name, especially their females.

HORN.    And cry, Horner's coming to carry you away. I am only afraid 'twill not be believed. You told 'em 'twas by an English-French disaster, and an English-French chirurgeon, who has given me at once not only a cure, but an antidote for the future against that damned malady, and that worse distemper, love, and all other women's evils?

QUACK.    Your late journey into France has made it the more credible, and your being here a fortnight before you appeared in public looks as if you apprehended the shame, which I wonder you do not. Well, I have been hired by young gallants to belie 'em t'other way, but you are the first would be thought a man unfit for women.

HORN.   Dear Mr. Doctor, let vain rogues be contented only to be thought abler men than they are; generally 'tis all the pleasure they have, but mine lies another way.

QUACK.   You take, methinks, a very preposterous way to it, and as ridiculous as if we operators in physic should put forth bills to disparage our medicaments, with hopes to gain customers.

HORN.   Doctor, there are quacks in love as well as physic, who get but the fewer and worse patients for their boasting; a good name is seldom got by giving it one's self; and women no more than honour are compassed by bragging. Come, come, Doctor, the wisest lawyer never discovers the merits of his cause till the trial; the wealthiest man conceals his riches, and the cunning gamester his play. Shy husbands and keepers, like old rooks, are not to be cheated but by a new unpractised trick: false friendship will pass now no more than false dice upon 'em; no, not in the city.

*Enter Boy*

BOY.   There are two ladies and a gentleman coming up.          [*exit*]

HORN.   A pox! some unbelieving sisters of my former acquaintance, who, I am afraid, expect their sense should be satisfied of the falsity of the report. No—this formal fool and women!

*Enter* SIR JASPER FIDGET, LADY FIDGET, *and* MRS. DAINTY FIDGET

QUACK.   His wife and sister.

SIR JASP.   My coach breaking just now before your door, Sir, I look upon as an occasional reprimand to me, Sir, for not kissing your hands, Sir, since your coming out of France, Sir; and so my disaster, Sir, has been my good fortune, Sir; and this is my wife and sister, Sir.

HORN.   What then, Sir?

SIR JASP.   My lady, and sister, Sir.—Wife, this is Master Horner.

LADY FID.   Master Horner, husband!

SIR JASP.   My lady, my Lady Fidget, Sir.

HORN.   So, Sir.

SIR JASP.   Won't you be acquainted with her, Sir?—[*aside*] So, the report is true, I find, by his coldness or aversion to the sex; but I'll play the wag with him.—Pray salute my wife, my lady, Sir.

HORN.   I will kiss no man's wife, Sir, for him, Sir; I have taken my eternal leave, Sir, of the sex already, Sir.

SIR JASP. [*aside*]   Ha! ha! ha! I'll plague him yet.——Not know my wife, Sir?

HORN.   I do not know your wife, Sir; she's a woman, Sir, and consequently a monster, Sir, a greater monster than a husband, Sir.

SIR JASP.   A husband! how, Sir?

HORN.    So, Sir; but I make no more cuckolds, Sir.         [*makes horns*]

SIR JASP.  Ha! ha! ha! Mercury! Mercury!

LADY FID.    Pray, Sir Jasper, let us be gone from this rude fellow.

MRS. DAIN.    Who, by his breeding, would think he had ever been in France?

LADY FID.    Foh! he's but too much a French fellow, such as hate women of quality and virtue for their love to their husbands, Sir Jasper; a woman is hated by 'em as much for loving her husband as for loving their money. But pray, let's be gone.

HORN.    You do well, Madam, for I have nothing that you came for: I have brought over not so much as a bawdy picture, no new postures, nor the second part of the *Escole des Filles;* nor——

QUACK. [*apart to* HORNER]    Hold, for shame, Sir! what d'ye mean? You will ruin yourself for ever with the sex——

SIR JASP.    Ha! ha! ha! he hates women perfectly, I find.

MRS. DAIN.    What pity 'tis he should!

LADY FID.    Ay, he's a base fellow for't. But affectation makes not a woman more odious to them than virtue.

HORN.    Because your virtue is your greatest affectation, Madam.

LADY FID.    How, you saucy fellow! would you wrong my honour?

HORN.    If I could.

LADY FID.    How d'ye mean, Sir?

SIR JASP.    Ha! ha! ha! no, he can't wrong your Ladyship's honour, upon my honour; he, poor man—hark you in your ear—a mere eunuch.

LADY FID.    O filthy French beast! foh! foh! why do we stay? let's be gone: I can't endure the sight of him.

SIR JASP.    Stay but till the chairs come; they'll be here presently.

LADY FID.    No, no.

SIR JASP.    Nor can I stay longer. 'Tis—let me see, a quarter and a half quarter of a minute past eleven. The council will be sat; I must away. Business must be preferred always before love and ceremony with the wise, Mr. Horner.

HORN.    And the impotent, Sir Jasper.

SIR JASP.    Ay, ay, the impotent, Master Horner; ha! ha! ha!

LADY FID.    What, leave us with a filthy man alone in his lodgings?

SIR JASP.    He's an innocent man now, you know. Pray stay, I'll hasten the chairs to you.—— Mr. Horner, your servant; I should be glad to see you at my house. Pray come and dine with me, and play at cards with my wife after dinner; you are fit for women at that game yet, ha! ha!—[*aside*] 'Tis as much a husband's prudence to provide innocent diversion for a wife as to hinder her unlawful pleasures; and he had better employ her than let her employ herself.—— Farewell.

HORN.    Your servant, Sir Jasper.

[*exit* SIR JASPER]

LADY FID.    I will not stay with him, foh!——

HORN.    Nay, Madam, I beseech you stay, if it be but to see I can be as civil to ladies yet as they would desire.

LADY FID.    No, no, foh! you cannot be civil to ladies.

MRS. DAIN.    You as civil as ladies would desire?

LADY FID.    No, no, no, foh! foh! foh!

[*exeunt* LADY FIDGET *and* MRS. DAINTY FIDGET]

QUACK.    Now, I think, I, or you yourself, rather, have done your business with the women.

HORN.    Thou art an ass. Don't you see already, upon the report and my carriage, this grave man of business leaves his wife in my lodgings, invites me to his house and wife, who before would not be acquainted with me out of jealousy?

QUACK.    Nay, by this means you may be the more acquainted with the husbands, but the less with the wives.

HORN.    Let me alone; if I can but abuse the husbands, I'll soon disabuse the wives. Stay—I'll reckon you up the advantages I am like to have by my stratagem. First, I shall be rid of all my old acquaintances, the most insatiable sorts of duns, that invade our lodgings in a morning; and next to the pleasure of making a new mistress is that of being rid of an old one, and of all old debts. Love, when it comes to be so, is paid the most unwillingly.

QUACK.    Well, you may be so rid of your old acquaintances; but how will you get any new ones?

HORN.    Doctor, thou wilt never make a good chemist, thou art so incredulous and impatient. Ask but all the young fellows of the town if they do not lose more time, like huntsmen, in starting the game, than in running it down. One knows not where to find 'em, who will or will not. Women of quality are so civil you can hardly distinguish love from good breeding, and a man is often mistaken: but now I can be sure she that shows an aversion to me loves the sport, as those women that are gone, whom I warrant to be right. And then the next thing is, your women of honour, as you call 'em, are only chary of their reputations, not their persons; and 'tis scandal they would avoid, not men. Now may I have, by the reputation of an eunuch, the privileges of one, and be seen in a lady's chamber in a morning as early as her husband; kiss virgins before their parents or lovers; and maybe, in short, the *passe-partout* of the town. Now, Doctor.

QUACK.    Nay, now you shall be the doctor, and your process is so new that we do not know but it may succeed.

HORN.    Not so new neither; *probatum est*, Doctor.

QUACK.    Well, I wish you luck, and many patients, whilst I go to mine.                                                                [*exit*]

*Enter* HARCOURT *and* DORILANT *to* HORNER

HAR. Come, your appearance at the play yesterday has, I hope, hardened you for the future against the women's contempt and the men's raillery; and now you'll abroad as you were wont.

HORN. Did I not bear it bravely?

DOR. With a most theatrical impudence, nay, more than the orange-wenches show there, or a drunken vizard-mask, or a great-bellied actress; nay, or the most impudent of creatures, an ill poet; or what is yet more impudent, a second-hand critic.

HORN. But what say the ladies? have they no pity?

HAR. What ladies? The vizard-masks, you know, never pity a man when all's gone, though in their service.

DOR. And for the women in the boxes, you'd never pity them when 'twas in your power.

HAR. They say 'tis pity but all that deal with common women should be served so.

DOR. Nay, I dare swear they won't admit you to play at cards with them, go to plays with 'em, or do the little duties which other shadows of men are wont to do for 'em.

HORN. What do you call shadows of men?

DOR. Half-men.

HORN. What, boys?

DOR. Ay, your old boys, old *beaux garçons*, who, like superannuated stallions, are suffered to run, feed, and whinny with the mares as long as they live, though they can do nothing else.

HORN. Well, a pox on love and wenching! Women serve but to keep a man from better company. Though I can't enjoy them, I shall you the more. Good fellowship and friendship are lasting, rational, and manly pleasures.

HAR. For all that, give me some of those pleasures you call effeminate too; they help to relish one another.

HORN. They disturb one another.

HAR. No, mistresses are like books. If you pore upon them too much, they doze you, and make you unfit for company; but if used discreetly, you are the fitter for conversation by 'em.

DOR. A mistress should be like a little country retreat near the town; not to dwell in constantly, but only for a night and away, to taste the town the better when a man returns.

HORN. I tell you, 'tis as hard to be a good fellow, a good friend, and a lover of women, as 'tis to be a good fellow, a good friend, and a lover of money. You cannot follow both, then choose your side. Wine gives you liberty, loves takes it away.

Dor.    Gad, he's in the right on't.

Horn.    Wine gives you joy; love, grief and tortures, besides the chirurgeon's. Wine makes us witty; love, only sots. Wine makes us sleep; love breaks it.

Dor.    By the world, he has reason, Harcourt.

Horn.    Wine makes——

Dor.    Ay, wine makes us—makes us princes; love makes us beggars, poor rogues, egad—and wine——

Horn.    So, there's one converted.—No, no, love and wine, oil and vinegar.

Har.    I grant it; love will still be uppermost.

Horn.    Come, for my part, I will have only those glorious manly pleasures of being very drunk and very slovenly.

*Enter Boy*

Boy.    Mr. Sparkish is below, Sir.                [*exit*]

Har.    What, my dear friend! a rogue that is fond of me, only I think, for abusing him.

Dor.    No, he can no more think the men laugh at him than that women jilt him, his opinion of himself is so good.

Horn.    Well, there's another pleasure by drinking I thought not of— I shall lose his acquaintance, because he cannot drink: and you know 'tis a very hard thing to be rid of him; for he's one of those nauseous offerers at wit, who, like the worst fiddlers, run themselves into all companies.

Har.    One that, by being in the company of men of sense, would pass for one.

Horn.    And may so to the short-sighted world, as a false jewel amongst true ones is not discerned at a distance. His company is as troublesome to us as a cuckold's when you have a mind to his wife's.

Har.    No, the rogue will not let us enjoy one another, but ravishes our conversation, though he signifies no more to't than Sir Martin Mar-all's gaping, and awkward thrumming upon the lute, does to his man's voice and music.

Dor.    And to pass for a wit in town shows himself a fool every night to us, that are guilty of the plot.

Horn.    Such wits as he are, to a company of reasonable men, like rooks to the gamesters, who only fill a room at the table, but are so far from contributing to the play, that they only serve to spoil the fancy of those that do.

Dor.    Nay, they are used like rooks too, snubbed, checked, and abused; yet the rogues will hang on.

Horn.    A pox on 'em, and all that force nature, and would be still what she forbids 'em! Affectation is her greatest monster.

HAR.    Most men are the contraries to that they would seem. Your bully, you see, is a coward with a long sword; the little humbly fawning physician, with his ebony cane, is he that destroys men.

DOR.    The usurer, a poor rogue, possessed of mouldy bonds and mortgages; and we they call spendthrifts are only wealthy who lay out his money upon daily new purchases of pleasure.

HORN.    Ay, your arrantest cheat is your trustee or executor, your jealous man, the greatest cuckold, your churchman the greatest atheist, and your noisy pert rogue of a wit, the greatest fop, dullest ass, and worst company, as you shall see; for here he comes.

*Enter* SPARKISH

SPARK.    How is't, sparks? how is't? Well, faith, Harry, I must rally thee a little, ha! ha! ha! upon the report in town of thee, ha! ha! ha! I can't hold i'faith; shall I speak?

HORN.    Yes; but you'll be so bitter then.

SPARK.    Honest Dick and Frank here shall answer for me, I will not be extreme bitter, by the universe.

HAR.    We will be bound in a ten-thousand-pound bond, he shall not be bitter at all.

DOR.    Nor sharp, nor sweet.

HORN.    What, not downright insipid?

SPARK.    Nay then, since you are so brisk, and provoke me, take what follows. You must know, I was discoursing and rallying with some ladies yesterday, and they happened to talk of the fine new signs in town.

HORN.    Very fine ladies, I believe.

SPARK.    Said I, I know where the best new sign is.—Where? says one of the ladies.—In Covent Garden, I replied.—Said another, In what street?—In Russel Street, answered I.—Lord, says another, I'm sure there was ne'er a fine new sign there yesterday.—Yes, but there was, said I again, and it came out of France, and has been there a fortnight.

DOR.    A pox! I can hear no more, prithee.

HORN.    No, hear him out; let him tune his crowd a while.

HAR.    The worst music, the greatest preparation.

SPARK.    Nay, faith, I'll make you laugh.—It cannot be, says a third lady.—Yes, yes, quoth I again.—Says a fourth lady——

HORN.    Look to't, we'll have no more ladies.

SPARK.    No—then mark, mark, now. Said I to the fourth, Did you never see Mr. Horner? he lodges in Russel Street, and he's a sign of a man, you know, since he came out of France; ha! ha! ha!

HORN.    But the devil take me if thine be the sign of a jest.

SPARK.    With that they all fell a-laughing, till they bepissed themselves. What, but it does not move you, methinks? Well, I see one had as good go to law without a witness, as break a jest without a laugher on one's side.——Come, come, sparks, but where do we dine? I have left at Whitehall an earl to dine with you.

DOR.   Why, I thought thou hadst loved a man with a title better than a suit with a French trimming to't.

HAR.   Go to him again.

SPARK.   No, Sir, a wit to me is the greatest title in the world.

HORN.   But go dine with your earl, Sir; he may be exceptious. We are your friends, and will not take it ill to be left, I do assure you.

HAR.   Nay, faith, he shall go to him.

SPARK.   Nay, pray, gentlemen.

DOR.   We'll thrust you out, if you won't; what, disappoint anybody for us?

SPARK.   Nay, dear gentlemen, hear me.

HORN.   No, no, Sir, by no means; pray go, Sir.

SPARK.   Why, dear rogues——

DOR.   No, no.                    [they all thrust him out of the room]

ALL.   Ha! ha! ha!

### SPARKISH *returns*

SPARK.   But, sparks, pray hear me. What, d'ye think I'll eat then with gay shallow fops and silent coxcombs? I think wit as necessary at dinner as a glass of good wine, and that's the reason I never have any stomach when I eat alone.—Come, but where do we dine?

HORN.   Even where you will.

SPARK.   At Chateline's?

DOR.   Yes, if you will.

SPARK.   Or at the Cock?

DOR.   Yes, if you please.

SPARK.   Or at the Dog and Partridge?

HORN.   Ay, if you have a mind to't; for we shall dine at neither.

SPARK.   Pshaw! with your fooling we shall lose the new play; and I would no more miss seeing a new play the first day, than I would miss sitting in the wits' row. Therefore I'll go fetch my mistress, and away.

[*exit*]

*Manent* HORNER, HARCOURT, DORILANT: *enter to them* MR. PINCHWIFE

HORN.   Who have we here? Pinchwife?

PINCH.   Gentlemen, your humble servant.

HORN.   Well, Jack, by thy long absence from the town, the grumness of thy countenance, and the slovenliness of thy habit, I should give thee joy, should I not, of marriage?

PINCH.   [*aside*]   Death! does he know I'm married too? I thought to have concealed it from him at least.——My long stay in the country will excuse my dress; and I have a suit of law that brings me up to town, that puts me out of humour. Besides, I must give Sparkish to-morrow five thousand pound to lie with my sister.

HORN.    Nay, you country gentlemen, rather than not purchase, will buy anything; and he is a cracked title, if we may quibble. Well, but am I to give thee joy? I heard thou wert married.

PINCH.    What then?

HORN.    Why, the next thing that is to be heard is, thou'rt a cuckold.

PINCH. [*aside*]    Insupportable name!

HORN.    But I did not expect marriage from such a whoremaster as you, one that knew the town so much, and women so well.

PINCH.    Why, I have married no London wife.

HORN.    Pshaw! that's all one. That grave circumspection in marrying a country wife, is like refusing a deceitful pampered Smithfield jade, to go and be cheated by a friend in the country.

PINCH. [*aside*]    A pox on him and his simile!——At least we are a little surer of the breed there, know what her keeping has been, whether foiled or unsound.

HORN.    Come, come, I have known a clap gotten in Wales; and there are cuzens, justices' clerks, and chaplains in the country, I won't say coachmen. But she's handsome and young?

PINCH. [*aside*]    I'll answer as I should do.——No, no; she has no beauty but her youth, no attraction but her modesty: wholesome, homely, and huswifely; that's all.

DOR.    He talks as like a grazier as he looks.

PINCH.    She's too awkward, ill-favoured, and silly to bring to town.

HAR.    Then methinks you should bring her to be taught breeding.

PINCH.    To be taught! no, Sir, I thank you. Good wives and private soldiers should be ignorant—I'll keep her from your instructions, I warrant you.

HAR. [*aside*]    The rogue is as jealous as if his wife were not ignorant.

HORN.    Why, if she be ill-favoured, there will be less danger here for you than by leaving her in the country. We have such variety of dainties that we are seldom hungry.

DOR.    But they have always coarse, constant, swingeing stomachs in the country.

HAR.    Foul feeders indeed!

DOR.    And your hospitality is great there.

HAR.    Open house; every man's welcome.

PINCH.    So, so, gentlemen.

HORN.    But prithee, why wouldst thou marry her? If she be ugly, ill-bred, and silly, she must be rich then.

PINCH.    As rich as if she brought me twenty thousand pound out of this town; for she'll be as sure not to spend her moderate portion as a London baggage would be to spend hers, let it be what it would: so 'tis all one. Then, because she's ugly, she's the likelier to be my own; and being ill-bred, she'll hate conversation; and since silly and innocent, will not know the difference betwixt a man of one-and-twenty and one of forty.

HORN.    Nine—to my knowledge. But if she be silly, she'll expect as much from a man of forty-nine, as from him of one-and-twenty. But me-thinks wit is more necessary than beauty; and I think no young woman ugly that has it, and no handsome woman agreeable without it.

PINCH.    'Tis my maxim, he's a fool that marries; but he's a greater that does not marry a fool. What is wit in a wife good for, but to make a man a cuckold?

HORN.    Yes, to keep it from his knowledge.

PINCH.    A fool cannot contrive to make her husband a cuckold.

HORN.    No; but she'll club with a man that can: and what is worse, if she cannot make her husband a cuckold, she'll make him jealous, and pass for one: and then 'tis all one.

PINCH.    Well, well, I'll take care for one. My wife shall make me no cuckold, though she had your help, Mr. Horner. I understand the town, Sir.

DOR. [aside]    His help!

HAR. [aside]    He's come newly to town, it seems, and has not heard how things are with him.

HORN.    But tell me, has marriage cured thee of whoring, which it seldom does?

HAR.    'Tis more than age can do.

HORN.    No, the word is, I'll marry and live honest: but a marriage vow is like a penitent gamester's oath, and entering into bonds and penalties to stint himself to such a particular small sum at play for the future, which makes him but the more eager; and not being able to hold out, loses his money again, and his forfeit to boot.

DOR.    Ay, ay, a gamester will be a gamester whilst his money lasts, and a whoremaster whilst his vigour.

HAR.    Nay, I have known 'em, when they are broke, and can lose no more, keep a-fumbling with the box in their hands to fool with only, and hinder other gamesters.

DOR.    That had wherewithal to make lusty stakes.

PINCH.    Well, gentlemen, you may laugh at me; but you shall never lie with my wife: I know the town.

HORN.    But prithee, was not the way you were in better? is not keeping better than marriage?

PINCH. A pox on't! the jades would jilt me, I could never keep a whore to myself.

HORN. So, then you only married to keep a whore to yourself. Well, but let me tell you, women, as you say, are like soldiers, made constant and loyal by good pay, rather than by oaths and covenants. Therefore I'd advise my friends to keep rather than marry, since too I find, by your example, it does not serve one's turn; for I saw you yesterday in the eighteen-penny place with a pretty country wench.

PINCH. [*aside*] How the devil! did he see my wife then? I sat there that she might not be seen. But she shall never go to a play again.

HORN. What! dost thou blush at nine-and-forty for having been seen with a wench?

DOR. No, faith, I warrant 'twas his wife, which he seated there out of sight; for he's a cunning rogue, and understands the town.

HAR. He blushes. Then 'twas his wife; for men are now more ashamed to be seen with them in public than with a wench.

PINCH. [*aside*] Hell and damnation! I'm undone, since Horner has seen her, and they know 'twas she.

HORN. But prithee, was it thy wife? She was exceedingly pretty: I was in love with her at that distance.

PINCH. You are like never to be nearer to her. Your servant, gentlemen. [*offers to go*]

HORN. Nay, prithee stay.

PINCH. I cannot; I will not.

HORN. Come, you shall dine with us.

PINCH. I have dined already.

HORN. Come, I know thou hast not: I'll treat thee, dear rogue; thou shalt spend none of thy Hampshire money to-day.

PINCH. [*aside*] Treat me! So, he uses me already like his cuckold.

HORN. Nay, you shall not go.

PINCH. I must; I have business at home. [*exit*]

HAR. To beat his wife. He's as jealous of her as a Cheapside husband of a Covent Garden wife.

HORN. Why, 'tis as hard to find an old whoremaster without jeal-ousy and the gout, as a young one without fear or the pox.

As gout in age from pox in youth proceeds,
So wenching past, then jealousy succeeds;
The worst disease that love and wenching breeds.

[*exeunt*]

# ACT II

MRS. MARGERY PINCHWIFE *and* ALITHEA.
PINCHWIFE *peeping behind at the door*

MRS. PINCH.   Pray, Sister, where are the best fields and woods to walk in, in London?

ALITH.   A pretty question!—Why, Sister, Mulberry Garden and St. James's Park; and, for close walks, the New Exchange.

MRS. PINCH.   Pray, Sister, tell me why my husband looks so grum here in town, and keeps me up so close, and will not let me go a-walking, nor let me wear my best gown yesterday.

ALITH.   Oh, he's jealous, Sister.

MRS. PINCH.   Jealous! what's that?

ALITH.   He's afraid you should love another man.

MRS. PINCH.   How should he be afraid of my loving another man, when he will not let me see any but himself?

ALITH.   Did he not carry you yesterday to a play?

MRS. PINCH.   Ay; but we sat amongst ugly people. He would not let me come near the gentry, who sat under us, so that I could not see 'em. He told me none but naughty women sat there, whom they toused and moused. But I would have ventured, for all that.

ALITH.   But how did you like the play?

MRS. PINCH.   Indeed I was weary of the play, but I liked hugeously the actors. They are the goodliest, properest men, Sister!

ALITH.   Oh, but you must not like the actors, Sister.

MRS. PINCH.   Ay, how should I help it, Sister? Pray, Sister, when my husband comes in, will you ask leave for me to go a-walking?

ALITH.   [*aside*]   A-walking! ha! ha! Lord, a country-gentlewoman's leisure is the drudgery of a footpost; and she requires as much airing as her husband's horses.——But here comes your husband: I'll ask, though I'm sure he'll not grant it.

MRS. PINCH.   He says he won't let me go abroad for fear of catching the pox.

ALITH.   Fy! the small-pox you should say.

15

*Enter* PINCHWIFE *to them*

MRS. PINCH.   O my dear, dear bud, welcome home! Why dost thou look so fropish? who has nangered thee?

PINCH.   You're a fool.          [MRS. PINCHWIFE *goes aside, and cries*]

ALITH.   Faith, so she is, for crying for no fault, poor tender creature!

PINCH.   What, you would have her as impudent as yourself, as arrant a jillflirt, a gadder, a magpie; and to say all, a mere notorious town-woman?

ALITH.   Brother, you are my only censurer; and the honour of your family will sooner suffer in your wife there than in me, though I take the innocent liberty of the town.

PINCH.   Hark you, mistress, do not talk so before my wife.—The innocent liberty of the town!

ALITH.   Why, pray, who boasts of any intrigue with me? what lampoon has made my name notorious? what ill women frequent my lodgings? I keep no company with any women of scandalous reputations.

PINCH.   No, you keep the men of scandalous reputations company.

ALITH.   Where? would you not have me civil? answer 'em in a box at the plays, in the drawing-room at Whitehall, in St. James's Park, Mulberry Garden, or——

PINCH.   Hold, hold! Do not teach my wife where the men are to be found: I believe she's the worse for your town-documents already. I bid you keep her in ignorance, as I do.

MRS. PINCH.   Indeed, be not angry with her, bud, she will tell me nothing of the town, though I ask her a thousand times a day.

PINCH.   Then you are very inquisitive to know, I find?

MRS. PINCH.   Not I indeed, dear; I hate London. Our place-house in the country is worth a thousand of 't: would I were there again!

PINCH.   So you shall, I warrant. But were you not talking of plays and players when I came in?——You are her encourager in such discourses.

MRS. PINCH.   No, indeed, dear; she chid me just now for liking the playermen.

PINCH. [*aside*]   Nay, if she be so innocent as to own to me her liking them, there is no hurt in't.——Come, my poor rogue, but thou lik'st none better than me?

MRS. PINCH.   Yes, indeed, but I do. The playermen are finer folks.

PINCH.   But you love none better than me?

MRS. PINCH.   You are my own dear bud, and I know you. I hate a stranger.

PINCH.   Ay, my dear, you must love me only, and not be like the naughty town-women, who only hate their husbands, and love every man else; love plays, visits, fine coaches, fine clothes, fiddles, balls, treats, and so lead a wicked town-life.

MRS. PINCH.  Nay, if to enjoy all these things be a town-life, London is not so bad a place, dear.

PINCH.  How! if you love me, you must hate London.

ALITH. [*aside*]  The fool has forbid me discovering to her the pleasures of the town, and he is now setting her agog upon them himself.

MRS. PINCH.  But, husband, do the town-women love the playermen too?

PINCH.  Yes, I warrant you.

MRS. PINCH.  Ay, I warrant you.

PINCH.  Why, you do not, I hope?

MRS. PINCH.  No, no, bud. But why have we no playermen in the country?

PINCH.  Ha!—Mrs. Minx, ask me no more to go to a play.

MRS. PINCH.  Nay, why love? I did not care for going: but when you forbid me, you make me, as 'twere, desire it.

ALITH. [*aside*]  So 'twill be in other things, I warrant.

MRS. PINCH.  Pray let me go to a play, dear.

PINCH.  Hold your peace, I wo' not.

MRS. PINCH.  Why, love?

PINCH.  Why, I'll tell you.

ALITH. [*aside*]  Nay, if he tell her, she'll give him more cause to forbid her that place.

MRS. PINCH.  Pray why, dear?

PINCH.  First, you like the actors; and the gallants may like you.

MRS. PINCH.  What, a homely country girl! No, bud, nobody will like me.

PINCH.  I tell you yes, they may.

MRS. PINCH.  No, no, you jest—I won't believe you: I will go.

PINCH.  I tell you then, that one of the lewdest fellows in town, who saw you there, told me he was in love with you.

MRS. PINCH.  Indeed! who, who, pray who was't?

PINCH. [*aside*]  I've gone too far, and slipped before I was aware; how overjoyed she is!

MRS. PINCH.  Was it any Hampshire gallant, any of our neighbours? I promise you, I am beholden to him.

PINCH.  I promise you, you lie; for he would but ruin you, as he has done hundreds. He has no other love for women but that; such as he look upon women, like basilisks, but to destroy 'em.

MRS. PINCH.  Ay, but if he loves me, why should he ruin me? answer me to that. Methinks he should not, I would do him no harm.

ALITH.  Ha! ha! ha!

PINCH.  'Tis very well; but I'll keep him from doing you any harm, or me either. But here comes company; get you in, get you in.

MRS. PINCH.   But, pray, husband, is he a pretty gentleman that loves me?

PINCH.   In, baggage, in.                    [*thrusts her in, shuts the door*]

*Enter* SPARKISH *and* HARCOURT

What, all the lewd libertines of the town brought to my lodging by this easy coxcomb! 'Sdeath, I'll not suffer it.

SPARK.   Here, Harcourt, do you approve my choice?——Dear little rogue, I told you I'd bring you acquainted with all my friends, the wits and——                    [HARCOURT *salutes her.*]

PINCH.   Ay, they shall know her, as well as you yourself will, I warrant you.

SPARK.   This is one of those, my pretty rogue, that are to dance at your wedding to-morrow; and him you must bid welcome ever, to what you and I have.

PINCH. [*aside*]   Monstrous!

SPARK.   Harcourt, how dost thou like her, faith? Nay, dear, do not look down; I should hate to have a wife of mine out of countenance at anything.

PINCH. [*aside*]   Wonderful!

SPARK.   Tell me, I say, Harcourt, how dost thou like her? Thou hast stared upon her enough to resolve me.

HAR.   So infinitely well, that I could wish I had a mistress too, that might differ from her in nothing but her love and engagement to you.

ALITH.   Sir, Master Sparkish has often told me that his acquaintance were all wits and railleurs, and now I find it.

SPARK.   No, by the universe, Madam, he does not rally now; you may believe him. I do assure you, he is the honestest, worthiest, true-hearted gentleman—a man of such perfect honour, he would say nothing to a lady he does not mean.

PINCH. [*aside*]   Praising another man to his mistress!

HAR.   Sir, you are so beyond expectation obliging, that——

SPARK.   Nay, egad, I am sure you do admire her extremely; I see't in your eyes.——He does admire you, Madam.——By the world, don't you?

HAR.   Yes, above the world, or the most glorious part of it, her whole sex: and till now I never thought I should have envied you, or any man about to marry, but you have the best excuse for marriage I ever knew.

ALITH.   Nay, now, Sir, I'm satisfied you are of the society of the wits and railleurs, since you cannot spare your friend, even when he is but too civil to you; but the surest sign is, since you are an enemy to marriage, for that I hear you hate as much as business or bad wine.

HAR.   Truly, Madam, I never was an enemy to marriage till now, because marriage was never an enemy to me before.

ALITH.  But why, Sir, is marriage an enemy to you now? Because it robs you of your friend here? for you look upon a friend married as one gone into a monastery, that is, dead to the world.

HAR.  'Tis indeed, because you marry him; I see, Madam, you can guess my meaning. I do confess heartily and openly I wish it were in my power to break the match; by Heavens I would.

SPARK.  Poor Frank!

ALITH.  Would you be so unkind to me?

HAR.  No, no, 'tis not because I would be unkind to you.

SPARK.  Poor Frank! no gad, 'tis only his kindness to me.

PINCH. [aside]  Great kindness to you indeed! Insensible fop, let a man make love to his wife to his face!

SPARK.  Come, dear Frank, for all my wife there, that shall be, thou shalt enjoy me sometimes, dear rogue. By my honour, we men of wit condole for our deceased brother in marriage, as much as for one dead in earnest: I think that was prettily said of me, ha, Harcourt?——But come, Frank, be not melancholy for me.

HAR.  No, I assure you, I am not melancholy for you.

SPARK.  Prithee, Frank, dost think my wife that shall be there, a fine person?

HAR.  I could gaze upon her till I became as blind as you are.

SPARK.  How as I am? how?

HAR.  Because you are a lover, and true lovers are blind, stock blind.

SPARK.  True, true; but by the world she has wit too, as well as beauty: go, go with her into a corner, and try if she has wit; talk to her anything; she's bashful before me.

HAR.  Indeed if a woman wants wit in a corner, she has it nowhere.

ALITH. [aside to SPARKISH]  Sir, you dispose of me a little before your time——

SPARK.  Nay, nay, Madam, let me have an earnest of your obedience, or—go, go, Madam——          [HARCOURT courts ALITHEA aside]

PINCH.  How, Sir! if you are not concerned for the honour of a wife, I am for that of a sister; he shall not debauch her. Be a pander to your own wife! bring men to her! let 'em make love before your face! thrust 'em into a corner together, then leave 'em in private! is this your town wit and conduct?

SPARK.  Ha! ha! ha! a silly wise rogue would make one laugh more than a stark fool, ha! ha! I shall burst. Nay, you shall not disturb 'em; I'll vex thee, by the world.

[struggles with PINCHWIFE to keep him from HARCOURT and ALITHEA]

ALITH.  The writings are drawn, Sir, settlements made: 'tis too late, Sir, and past all revocation.

HAR.  Then so is my death.

ALITH. I would not be unjust to him.

HAR. Then why to me so?

ALITH. I have no obligation to you.

HAR. My love.

ALITH. I had his before.

HAR. You never had it; he wants, you see, jealousy, the only infallible sign of it.

ALITH. Love proceeds from esteem; he cannot distrust my virtue: besides, he loves me, or he would not marry me.

HAR. Marrying you is no more sign of his love than bribing your woman, that he may marry you, is a sign of his generosity. Marriage is rather a sign of interest than love; and he that marries a fortune covets a mistress, not loves her. But if you take marriage for a sign of love, take it from me immediately.

ALITH. No, now you have put a scruple in my head; but in short, Sir, to end our dispute, I must marry him; my reputation would suffer in the world else.

HAR. No; if you do marry him, with your pardon, Madam, your reputation suffers in the world, and you would be thought in necessity for a cloak.

ALITH. Nay, now you are rude, Sir.——Mr. Sparkish, pray come hither, your friend here is very troublesome, and very loving.

HAR. [*aside to* ALITHEA] Hold! hold!——

PINCH. D'ye hear that?

SPARK. Why, d'ye think I'll seem to be jealous, like a country bumpkin?

PINCH. No, rather be a cuckold, like a credulous cit.

HAR. Madam, you would not have been so little generous as to have told him.

ALITH. Yes, since you could be so little generous as to wrong him.

HAR. Wrong him! no man can do't, he's beneath an injury: a bubble, a coward, a senseless idiot, a wretch so contemptible to all the world but you, that——

ALITH. Hold, do not rail at him, for since he is like to be my husband, I am resolved to like him: nay, I think I am obliged to tell him you are not his friend.——Master Sparkish, Master Sparkish!

SPARK. What, what?——Now, dear rogue, has not she wit?

HAR. Not so much as I thought, and hoped she had. [*speaks surlily*]

ALITH. Mr. Sparkish, do you bring people to rail at you?

HAR. Madam——

SPARK. How! no; but if he does rail at me, 'tis but in jest, I warrant: what we wits do for one another, and never take any notice of it.

ALITH. He spoke so scurrilously of you, I had no patience to hear him; besides, he has been making love to me.

HAR. [aside]   True, damned tell-tale woman!

SPARK.   Pshaw! to show his parts—we wits rail and make love often, but to show our parts: as we have no affections, so we have no malice, we——

ALITH.   He said you were a wretch below an injury——

SPARK.   Pshaw!

HAR. [aside]   Damned, senseless, impudent, virtuous jade! Well, since she won't let me have her, she'll do as good, she'll make me hate her.

ALITH.   A common bubble——

SPARK.   Pshaw!

ALITH.   A coward——

SPARK.   Pshaw, pshaw!

ALITH.   A senseless, drivelling idiot——

SPARK.   How! did he disparage my parts? Nay, then, my honour's concerned, I can't put up that, Sir, by the world—brother, help me to kill him.—[aside] I may draw now, since we have the odds of him—'tis a good occasion, too, before my mistress—— [offers to draw]

ALITH.   Hold, hold!

SPARK.   What, what?

ALITH. [aside]   I must not let 'em kill the gentleman neither, for his kindness to me: I am so far from hating him, that I wish my gallant had his person and understanding. Nay, if my honour——

SPARK.   I'll be thy death.

ALITH.   Hold, hold! Indeed, to tell the truth, the gentleman said after all, that what he spoke was but out of friendship to you.

SPARK.   How! say, I am—I am a fool, that is no wit, out of friendship to me?

ALITH.   Yes, to try whether I was concerned enough for you; and made love to me only to be satisfied of my virtue, for your sake.

HAR. [aside]   Kind, however.

SPARK.   Nay, if it were so, my dear rogue, I ask thee pardon; but why would not you tell me so, faith?

HAR.   Because I did not think on't, faith.

SPARK.   Come, Horner does not come; Harcourt, let's be gone to the new play.—Come, Madam.

ALITH.   I will not go, if you intend to leave me alone in the box and run into the pit, as you use to do.

SPARK.   Pshaw! I'll leave Harcourt with you in the box to entertain you, and that's as good; if I sat in the box, I should be thought no judge but of trimmings.—Come away, Harcourt, lead her down.

[exeunt SPARKISH, HARCOURT, and ALITHEA]

PINCH.   Well, go thy ways, for the flower of the true town fops, such as spend their estates before they come to 'em, and are cuckolds before they're married. But let me go look to my own freehold.—How!

*Enter* MY LADY FIDGET, MRS. DAINTY FIDGET, *and* MRS. SQUEAMISH

LADY FID.　Your servant, Sir: where is your lady? We are come to wait upon her to the new play.

PINCH.　New play!

LADY FID.　And my husband will wait upon you presently.

PINCH. [*aside*]　Damn your civility.——Madam, by no means; I will not see Sir Jasper here till I have waited upon him at home; nor shall my wife see you till she has waited upon your ladyship at your lodgings.

LADY FID.　Now we are here, Sir?

PINCH.　No, Madam.

MRS. DAIN.　Pray, let us see her.

MRS. SQUEAM.　We will not stir till we see her.

PINCH. [*aside*]　A pox on you all!—[*goes to the door, and returns*] She has locked the door, and is gone abroad.

LADY FID.　No, you have locked the door, and she's within.

MRS. DAIN.　They told us below she was here.

PINCH. [*aside*]　Will nothing do?——Well, it must out then. To tell you the truth, ladies, which I was afraid to let you know before, lest it might endanger your lives, my wife has just now the small-pox come out upon her; do not be frightened, but pray be gone, ladies; you shall not stay here in danger of your lives; pray get you gone, ladies.

LADY FID.　No, no, we have all had 'em.

MRS. SQUEAM.　Alack, alack!

MRS. DAIN.　Come, come, we must see how it goes with her; I understand the disease.

LADY FID.　Come!

PINCH. [*aside*]　Well, there is no being too hard for women at their own weapon, lying, therefore I'll quit the field.　　　　　　[*exit*]

MRS. SQUEAM.　Here's an example of jealousy!

LADY FID.　Indeed, as the world goes, I wonder there are no more jealous, since wives are so neglected.

MRS. DAIN.　Pshaw! as the world goes, to what end should they be jealous?

LADY FID.　Foh! 'tis a nasty world.

MRS. SQUEAM.　That men of parts, great acquaintance, and quality, should take up with and spend themselves and fortunes in keeping little playhouse creatures, foh!

LADY FID.　Nay, that women of understanding, great acquaintance, and good quality, should fall a-keeping too of little creatures, foh!

MRS. SQUEAM.　Why, 'tis the men of quality's fault; they never visit women of honour and reputation as they used to do; and have not so much as common civility for ladies of our rank, but use us with the same indifferency and ill-breeding as if we were all married to 'em.

LADY FID.    She says true; 'tis an arrant shame women of quality should be so slighted; methinks birth—birth should go for something; I have known men admired, courted, and followed for their titles only.

MRS. SQUEAM.    Ay, one would think men of honour should not love, no more than marry, out of their own rank.

MRS. DAIN.    Fy, fy, upon 'em! they are come to think cross breeding for themselves best, as well as for their dogs and horses.

LADY FID.    They are dogs and horses for't.

MRS. SQUEAM.    One would think, if not for love, for vanity a little.

MRS. DAIN.    Nay, they do satisfy their vanity upon us sometimes; and are kind to us in their report, tell all the world they lie with us.

LADY FID.    Damned rascals, that we should be only wronged by 'em! To report a man has had a person, when he has not had a person, is the greatest wrong in the whole world that can be done to a person.

MRS. SQUEAM.    Well, 'tis an arrant shame noble persons should be so wronged and neglected.

LADY FID.    But still 'tis an arranter shame for a noble person to neglect her own honour, and defame her own noble person with little inconsiderable fellows, foh!

MRS. DAIN.    I suppose the crime against our honour is the same with a man of quality as with another.

LADY FID.    How! no, sure, the man of quality is likest one's husband, and therefore the fault should be the less.

MRS. DAIN.    But then the pleasure should be the less.

LADY FID.    Fy, fy, fy, for shame, Sister! whither shall we ramble? Be continent in your discourse, or I shall hate you.

MRS. DAIN.    Besides, an intrigue is so much the more notorious for the man's quality.

MRS. SQUEAM.    'Tis true, that nobody takes notice of a private man, and therefore with him 'tis more secret; and the crime's the less when 'tis not known.

LADY FID.    You say true; i'faith, I think you are in the right on't: 'tis not an injury to a husband till it be an injury to our honours; so that a woman of honour loses no honour with a private person; and to say truth——

MRS. DAIN. [apart to MRS. SQUEAMISH]    So, the little fellow is grown a private person—with her——

LADY FID.    But still my dear, dear honour——

*Enter* SIR JASPER, HORNER, *and* DORILANT

SIR JASP. Ay, my dear, dear of honour, thou hast still so much honour in thy mouth——

HORN. [*aside*]  That she has none elsewhere.

LADY FID.  Oh, what d'ye mean to bring in these upon us?

MRS. DAIN.  Foh! these are as bad as wits.

MRS. SQUEAM.  Foh!

LADY FID.  Let us leave the room.

SIR JASP.  Stay, stay; faith, to tell you the naked truth——

LADY FID.  Fy, Sir Jasper! do not use that word naked.

SIR JASP.  Well, well, in short I have business at Whitehall, and cannot go to the play with you, therefore would have you go——

LADY FID.  With those two to a play?

SIR JASP.  No, not with t'other, but with Mr. Horner; there can be no more scandal to go with him than with Mr. Tattle, or Master Limberham.

LADY FID.  With that nasty fellow! no—no.

SIR JASP.  Nay, prithee, dear, hear me.  [*whispers to* LADY FIDGET]

HORN.  Ladies——

[HORNER, DORILANT *drawing near* MRS. SQUEAMISH *and* MRS. DAINTY FIDGET]

MRS. DAIN.  Stand off.

MRS. SQUEAM.  Do not approach us.

MRS. DAIN.  You herd with the wits, you are obscenity all over.

MRS. SQUEAM.  And I would as soon look upon a picture of Adam and Eve without fig-leaves, as any of you, if I could help it; therefore keep off, and do not make us sick.

DOR.  What a devil are these?

HORN.  Why, these are pretenders to honour, as critics to wit, only by censuring others; and as every raw, peevish, out-of-humoured, affected, dull, tea-drinking, arithmetical fop, sets up for a wit by railing at men of sense, so these for honour, by railing at the court, and ladies of as great honour as quality.

SIR JASP.  Come, Mr. Horner, I must desire you to go with these ladies to the play, Sir.

HORN.  I, Sir?

SIR JASP.  Ay, ay, come, Sir.

HORN.  I must beg your pardon, Sir, and theirs; I will not be seen in women's company in public again for the world.

SIR JASP.  Ha, ha, strange aversion!

MRS. SQUEAM.  No, he's for women's company in private.

SIR JASP.  He—poor man—he—ha! ha! ha!

MRS. DAIN.  'Tis a greater shame amongst lewd fellows to be seen in virtuous women's company, than for the women to be seen with them.

HORN.  Indeed, Madam, the time was I only hated virtuous women, but now I hate the other too; I beg your pardon, ladies.

LADY FID.   You are very obliging, Sir, because we would not be troubled with you.

SIR JASP.   In sober sadness, he shall go.

DOR.   Nay, if he wo' not, I am ready to wait upon the ladies, and I think I am the fitter man.

SIR JASP.   You, Sir! no, I thank you for that. Master Horner is a privileged man amongst the virtuous ladies, 'twill be a great while before you are so; he! he! he! he's my wife's gallant; he! he! he! No, pray withdraw, Sir, for as I take it, the virtuous ladies have no business with you.

DOR.   And I am sure he can have none with them. 'Tis strange a man can't come amongst virtuous women now, but upon the same terms as men are admitted into the Great Turk's seraglio. But heavens keep me from being an ombre player with 'em!——But where is Pinchwife?

[exit]

SIR JASP.   Come, come, man; what, avoid the sweet society of womankind? that sweet, soft, gentle, tame, noble creature, woman, made for man's companion——

HORN.   So is that soft, gentle, tame, and more noble creature a spaniel, and has all their tricks; can fawn, lie down, suffer beating, and fawn the more; barks at your friends when they come to see you, makes your bed hard, gives you fleas, and the mange sometimes. And all the difference is, the spaniel's the more faithful animal, and fawns but upon one master.

SIR JASP.   He! he! he!

MRS. SQUEAM.   Oh the rude beast!

MRS. DAIN.   Insolent brute!

LADY FID.   Brute! stinking, mortified, rotten French wether, to dare——

SIR JASP.   Hold, an't please your ladyship.——For shame, Master Horner! your mother was a woman—[aside] Now shall I never reconcile 'em.——[aside to LADY FIDGET] Hark you, Madam, take my advice in your anger. You know you often want one to make up your drolling pack of ombre players, and you may cheat him easily; for he's an ill gamester, and consequently loves play. Besides, you know you have but two old civil gentlemen (with stinking breaths too) to wait upon you abroad; take in the third into your service. The others are but crazy; and a lady should have a supernumerary gentleman-usher as a supernumerary coach-horse, lest sometimes you should be forced to stay at home.

LADY FID.   But are you sure he loves play, and has money?

SIR JASP.   He loves play as much as you, and has money as much as I.

LADY FID.   Then I am contented to make him pay for his scurrility. Money makes up in a measure all other wants in men.—Those whom we cannot make hold for gallants, we make fine.

SIR JASP. [*aside*]   So, so; now to mollify, wheedle him.——[*aside to* HORNER] Master Horner, will you never keep civil company? Methinks 'tis time now, since you are only fit for them. Come, come, man, you must e'en fall to visiting our wives, eating at our tables, drinking tea with our virtuous relations after dinner, dealing cards to 'em, reading plays and gazettes to 'em, picking fleas out of their shocks for 'em, collecting receipts, new songs, women, pages, and footmen for 'em.

HORN.   I hope they'll afford me better employment, Sir.

SIR JASP.   He! he! he! 'tis fit you know your work before you come into your place. And since you are unprovided of a lady to flatter, and a good house to eat at, pray frequent mine, and call my wife mistress, and she shall call you gallant, according to the custom.

HORN.   Who, I?

SIR JASP.   Faith, thou shalt for my sake; come, for my sake only.

HORN.   For your sake——

SIR JASP.   Come, come, here's a gamester for you; let him be a little familiar sometimes; nay, what if a little rude? Gamesters may be rude with ladies, you know.

LADY FID.   Yes; losing gamesters have a privilege with women.

HORN.   I always thought the contrary, that the winning gamester had most privilege with women; for when you have lost your money to a man, you'll lose anything you have, all you have, they say, and he may use you as he pleases.

SIR JASP.   He! he! he! well, win or lose, you shall have your liberty with her.

LADY FID.   As he behaves himself; and for your sake I'll give him admittance and freedom.

HORN.   All sorts of freedom, Madam?

SIR JASP.   Ay, ay, ay, all sorts of freedom thou canst take. And so go to her, begin thy new employment; wheedle her, jest with her, and be better acquainted one with another.

HORN. [*aside*]   I think I know her already; therefore may venture with her my secret for hers.          [HORNER *and* LADY FIDGET *whisper*]

SIR JASP.   Sister, cuz, I have provided an innocent playfellow for you there.

MRS. DAIN.   Who, he?

MRS. SQUEAM.   There's a playfellow, indeed!

SIR JASP.   Yes, sure. What, he is good enough to play at cards, blind-man's-buff, or the fool with, sometimes!

MRS. SQUEAM.   Foh! we'll have no such playfellows.

MRS. DAIN.   No, Sir; you shan't choose playfellows for us, we thank you.

SIR JASP.    Nay, pray hear me.                    [*whispering to them*]

LADY FID.    But, poor gentleman, could you be so generous, so truly a man of honour, as for the sakes of us women of honour, to cause yourself to be reported no man? No man! and to suffer yourself the greatest shame that could fall upon a man, that none might fall upon us women by your conversation? But, indeed, Sir, as perfectly, perfectly the same man as before your going into France, Sir? as perfectly, perfectly, Sir?

HORN.    As perfectly, perfectly, Madam. Nay, I scorn you should take my word; I desire to be tried only, Madam.

LADY FID.    Well, that's spoken again like a man of honour: all men of honour desire to come to the test. But, indeed, generally you men report such things of yourselves, one does not know how or whom to believe; and it is come to that pass we dare not take your words no more than your tailor's, without some staid servant of yours be bound with you. But I have so strong a faith in your honour, dear, dear, noble Sir, that I'd forfeit mine for yours, at any time, dear Sir.

HORN.    No, Madam, you should not need to forfeit it for me; I have given you security already to save you harmless, my late reputation being so well known in the world, Madam.

LADY FID.    But if upon any future falling-out, or upon a suspicion of my taking the trust out of your hands to employ some other, you yourself should betray your trust, dear Sir? I mean, if you'll give me leave to speak obscenely, you might tell, dear Sir.

HORN.    If I did, nobody would believe me. The reputation of impotency is as hardly recovered again in the world as that of cowardice, dear Madam.

LADY FID.    Nay, then, as one may say, you may do your worst, dear, dear Sir.

SIR JASP.    Come, is your ladyship reconciled to him yet? have you agreed on matters? For I must be gone to Whitehall.

LADY FID.    Why, indeed, Sir Jasper, Master Horner is a thousand, thousand times a better man than I thought him. Cousin Squeamish, sister Dainty, I can name him now. Truly, not long ago, you know, I thought his very name obscenity; and I would as soon have lain with him as have named him.

SIR JASP.    Very likely, poor Madam.

MRS. DAIN.    I believe it.

MRS. SQUEAM.    No doubt on't.

SIR JASP.    Well, well—that your ladyship is as virtuous as any she, I know, and him all the town knows—he! he! he! Therefore now you like him, get you gone to your business together; go, go to your business, I say, pleasure; whilst I go to my pleasure, business.

LADY FID.    Come, then, dear gallant.

HORN.    Come away, my dearest mistress.

SIR JASP.    So, so; why, 'tis as I'd have it.                    [*exit*]

HORN.    And as I'd have it.

LADY FID.    Who for his business from his wife will run,
Takes the best care to have her business done.

[*exeunt omnes*]

# ACT III

## SCENE I

### ALITHEA and MRS. PINCHWIFE

ALITH. Sister, what ails you? You are grown melancholy.

MRS. PINCH. Would it not make any one melancholy to see you go every day fluttering about abroad, whilst I must stay at home like a poor lonely sullen bird in a cage?

ALITH. Ay, Sister, but you came young, and just from the nest to your cage, so that I thought you liked it, and could be as cheerful in't as others that took their flight themselves early, and are hopping abroad in the open air.

MRS. PINCH. Nay, I confess I was quiet enough till my husband told me what pure lives the London ladies live abroad, with their dancing, meetings, and junketings, and dressed every day in their best gowns; and I warrant you, play at nine-pins every day of the week, so they do.

### Enter PINCHWIFE

PINCH. Come, what's here to do? You are putting the town-pleasures in her head, and setting her a-longing.

ALITH. Yes, after nine-pins. You suffer none to give her those longings you mean but yourself.

PINCH. I tell her of the vanities of the town like a confessor.

ALITH. A confessor! just such a confessor as he that, by forbidding a silly ostler to grease the horse's teeth, taught him to do't.

PINCH. Come, Mistress Flippant, good precepts are lost when bad examples are still before us: the liberty you take abroad makes her hanker after it, and out of humour at home. Poor wretch! she desired not to come to London; I would bring her.

ALITH. Very well.

PINCH. She has been this week in town, and never desired till this afternoon to go abroad.

ALITH. Was she not at a play yesterday?

29

PINCH.    Yes, but she ne'er asked me; I was myself the cause of her going.

ALITH.    Then if she ask you again, you are the cause of her asking, and not my example.

PINCH.    Well, to-morrow night I shall be rid of you; and the next day, before 'tis light, she and I'll be rid of the town, and my dreadful apprehensions.——Come, be not melancholy; for thou shalt go into the country after to-morrow, dearest.

ALITH.    Great comfort!

MRS. PINCH.    Pish! what d'ye tell me of the country for?

PINCH.    How's this! what, pish at the country?

MRS. PINCH.    Let me alone; I am not well.

PINCH.    Oh, if that be all—what ails my dearest?

MRS. PINCH.    Truly, I don't know: but I have not been well since you told me there was a gallant at the play in love with me.

PINCH.    Ha!——

ALITH.    That's by my example too!

PINCH.    Nay, if you are not well, but are so concerned because a lewd fellow chanced to lie, and say he liked you, you'll make me sick too.

MRS. PINCH.    Of what sickness?

PINCH.    Oh, of that which is worse than the plague, jealousy.

MRS. PINCH.    Pish, you jeer! I'm sure there's no such disease in our receipt-book at home.

PINCH.    No, thou never met'st with it, poor innocent.—[*aside*] Well, if thou cuckold me, 'twill be my own fault—for cuckolds and bastards are generally makers of their own fortune.

MRS. PINCH.    Well, but pray, bud, let's go to a play to-night.

PINCH.    'Tis just done, she comes from it. But why are you so eager to see a play?

MRS. PINCH.    Faith, dear, not that I care one pin for their talk there; but I like to look upon the playermen, and would see, if I could, the gallant you say loves me: that's all, dear bud.

PINCH.    Is that all, dear bud?

ALITH.    This proceeds from my example!

MRS. PINCH.    But if the play be done, let's go abroad, however, dear bud.

PINCH.    Come, have a little patience and thou shalt go into the country on Friday.

MRS. PINCH.    Therefore I would see first some sights to tell my neighbours of. Nay, I will go abroad, that's once.

ALITH.    I'm the cause of this desire too!

PINCH.    But now I think on't, who, who was the cause of Horner's coming to my lodgings to-day? That was you.

ALITH.    No, you, because you would not let him see your handsome wife out of your lodging.

MRS. PINCH.    Why, O Lord! did the gentleman come hither to see me indeed?

PINCH.    No, no. You are not the cause of that damned question too, Mistress Alithea?—[*aside*] Well, she's in the right of it. He is in love with my wife—and comes after her—'tis so—but I'll nip his love in the bud, lest he should follow us into the country, and break his chariot-wheel near our house, on purpose for an excuse to come to't. But I think I know the town.

MRS. PINCH.    Come, pray, bud, let's go abroad before 'tis late; for I will go, that's flat and plain.

PINCH. [*aside*]    So! the obstinacy already of the town-wife; and I must, whilst she's here, humour her like one.——Sister, how shall we do, that she may not be seen or known?

ALITH.    Let her put on her mask.

PINCH.    Pshaw! a mask makes people but the more inquisitive, and is as ridiculous a disguise as a stage-beard: her shape, stature, habit will be known. And if we should meet with Horner, he would be sure to take acquaintance with us, must wish her joy, kiss her, talk to her, leer upon her, and the devil and all. No, I'll not use her to a mask, 'tis dangerous, for masks have made more cuckolds than the best faces that ever were known.

ALITH.    How will you do then?

MRS. PINCH.    Nay, shall we go? The Exchange will be shut, and I have a mind to see that.

PINCH.    So—I have it—I'll dress her up in the suit we are to carry down to her brother, little Sir James; nay, I understand the town-tricks. Come, let's go dress her. A mask! no—a woman masked, like a covered dish, gives a man curiosity and appetite; when, it may be, uncovered, 'twould turn his stomach: no, no.

ALITH.    Indeed your comparison is something a greasy one: but I had a gentle gallant used to say, A beauty masked, like the sun in eclipse, gathers together more gazers than if it shined out.          [*exeunt*]

# SCENE II

*The Scene Changes to the New Exchange*

*Enter* HORNER, HARCOURT, *and* DORILANT

DOR.    Engaged to women, and not sup with us!

HORN.    Ay, a pox on 'em all!

HAR.    You were much a more reasonable man in the morning, and had as noble resolutions against 'em as a widower of a week's liberty.

DOR.   Did I ever think to see you keep company with women in vain?

HORN.   In vain: no—'tis since I can't love 'em, to be revenged on 'em.

HAR.   Now your sting is gone, you looked in the box amongst all those women like a drone in the hive, all upon you; shoved and ill-used by 'em all, and thrust from one side to t'other.

DOR.   Yet he must be buzzing amongst 'em still, like other beetle-headed liquorish drones. Avoid 'em, and hate 'em, as they hate you.

HORN.   Because I do hate 'em, and would hate 'em yet more, I'll frequent 'em. You may see by marriage, nothing makes a man hate a woman more than her constant conversation. In short, I converse with 'em, as you do with rich fools, to laugh at 'em and use 'em ill.

DOR.   But I would no more sup with women unless I could lie with 'em than sup with a rich coxcomb unless I could cheat him.

HORN.   Yes, I have known thee sup with a fool for his drinking; if he could set out your hand that way only, you were satisfied, and if he were a wine-swallowing mouth, 'twas enough.

HAR.   Yes, a man drinks often with a fool, as he tosses with a marker, only to keep his hand in use. But do the ladies drink?

HORN.   Yes, Sir; and I shall have the pleasure at least of laying 'em flat with a bottle, and bring as much scandal that way upon 'em as formerly t'other.

HAR.   Perhaps you may prove as weak a brother amongst 'em that way as t'other.

DOR.   Foh! drinking with women is as unnatural as scolding with 'em. But 'tis a pleasure of decayed fornicators, and the basest way of quenching love.

HAR.   Nay, 'tis drowning love, instead of quenching it. But leave us for civil women too!

DOR.   Ay, when he can't be the better for 'em. We hardly pardon a man that leaves his friend for a wench, and that's a pretty lawful call.

HORN.   Faith, I would not leave you for 'em, if they would not drink.

DOR.   Who would disappoint his company at Lewis's for a gossiping?

HAR.   Foh! Wine and women, good apart, together as nauseous as sack and sugar. But hark you, Sir, before you go, a little of your advice; an old maimed general, when unfit for action, is fittest for counsel. I have other designs upon women than eating and drinking with them; I am in love with Sparkish's mistress, whom he is to marry to-morrow: now how shall I get her?

*Enter* SPARKISH, *looking about*

HORN.　Why, here comes one will help you to her.

HAR.　He! he, I tell you, is my rival, and will hinder my love.

HORN.　No; a foolish rival and a jealous husband assist their rival's designs, for they are sure to make their women hate them, which is the first step to their love for another man.

HAR.　But I cannot come near his mistress but in his company.

HORN.　Still the better for you; for fools are most easily cheated when they themselves are accessories, and he is to be bubbled of his mistress as of his money, the common mistress, by keeping him company.

SPARK.　Who is that that is to be bubbled? Faith, let me snack; I han't met with a bubble since Christmas. 'Gad, I think bubbles are like their brother woodcocks, go out with the cold weather.

HAR. [*apart to* HORNER]　A pox! he did not hear all, I hope.

SPARK.　Come, you bubbling rogues you, where do we sup?——Oh, Harcourt, my mistress tells me you have been making fierce love to her all the play long: ha! ha! But I——

HAR.　I make love to her!

SPARK.　Nay, I forgive thee, for I think I know thee, and I know her; but I am sure I know myself.

HAR.　Did she tell you so? I see all women are like these of the Exchange; who, to enhance the prize of their commodities, report to their fond customers offers which were never made 'em.

HORN.　Ay, women are apt to tell before the intrigue, as men after it, and so show themselves the vainer sex. But hast thou a mistress, Sparkish? 'Tis as hard for me to believe it as that thou ever hadst a bubble, as you bragged just now.

SPARK.　Oh, your servant, Sir: are you at your raillery, Sir? But we were some of us beforehand with you to-day at the play. The wits were something bold with you, Sir; did you not hear us laugh?

HORN.　Yes; but I thought you had gone to plays to laugh at the poet's wit, not at your own.

SPARK.　Your servant, Sir: no, I thank you. 'Gad, I go to a play as to a country treat; I carry my own wine to one, and my own wit to t'other, or else I'm sure I should not be merry at either. And the reason why we are so often louder than the players is because we think we speak more wit, and so become the poet's rivals in his audience: for to tell you the truth, we hate the silly rogues, nay, so much, that we find fault even with their bawdy upon the stage, whilst we talk nothing else in the pit as loud.

HORN.　· But why shouldst thou hate the silly poets? Thou hast too much wit to be one; and they, like whores, are only hated by each other: and thou dost scorn writing, I'm sure.

SPARK.　Yes; I'd have you to know I scorn writing: but women, women, that make men do all foolish things, make 'em write songs too.

Everybody does it. 'Tis even as common with lovers as playing with fans; and you can no more help rhyming to your Phyllis, than drinking to your Phyllis.

HAR.    Nay, poetry in love is no more to be avoided than jealousy.

DOR.    But the poets damned your songs, did they?

SPARK.    Damn the poets! they turned 'em into burlesque, as they call it. That burlesque is a hocus-pocus trick they have got, which, by the virtue of *Hictius doctius, topsy turvy,* they make a wise and witty man in the world, a fool upon the stage you know not how: and 'tis therefore I hate 'em too, for I know not but it may be my own case; for they'll put a man into a play for looking asquint. Their predecessors were contented to make serving-men only their stage-fools: but these rogues must have gentlemen, with a pox to 'em, nay, knights; and, indeed, you shall hardly see a fool upon the stage but he's a knight. And to tell you the truth, they have kept me these six years from being a knight in earnest, for fear of being knighted in a play, and dubbed a fool.

DOR.    Blame 'em not, they must follow their copy, the age.

HAR.    But why shouldst thou be afraid of being in a play, who expose yourself every day in the playhouses, and at public places?

HORN.    'Tis but being on the stage, instead of standing on a bench in the pit.

DOR.    Don't you give money to painters to draw you like? and are you afraid of your pictures at length in a playhouse, where all your mistresses may see you?

SPARK.    A pox! painters don't draw the small-pox or pimples in one's face. Come, damn all your silly authors whatever, all books and booksellers, by the world, and all readers, courteous or uncourteous!

HAR.    But who comes here, Sparkish?

*Enter* MR. PINCHWIFE *and his Wife in man's clothes,*
ALITHEA, LUCY *her maid*

SPARK.    Oh, hide me! There's my mistress too.

            [SPARKISH *hides himself behind* HARCOURT]

HAR.    She sees you.

SPARK.    But I will not see her. 'Tis time to go to Whitehall, and I must not fail the drawing-room.

HAR.    Pray, first carry me, and reconcile me to her.

SPARK.    Another time. Faith, the king will have supped.

HAR.    Not with the worse stomach for thy absence. Thou art one of those fools that think their attendance at the king's meals as necessary as his physicians' when you are more troublesome to him than his doctors or his dogs.

SPARK.    Pshaw! I know my interest, Sir. Prithee hide me.

HORN.    Your servant, Pinchwife.——What, he knows us not!

PINCH. [*to his wife aside*]    Come along.

MRS. PINCH.    Pray, have you any ballads? give me sixpenny worth.

CLASP.    We have no ballads.

MRS. PINCH.    Then give me "Covent Garden Drollery," and a play or two—— Oh, here's "Tarugo's Wiles," and "The Slighted Maiden"; I'll have them.

PINCH. [*apart to her*]    No; plays are not for your reading. Come along; will you discover yourself?

HORN.    Who is that pretty youth with him, Sparkish?

SPARK.    I believe his wife's brother, because he's something like her: but I never saw her but once.

HORN.    Extremely handsome; I have seen a face like it too. Let us follow 'em.             [*exeunt* PINCHWIFE, MRS. PINCHWIFE, ALITHEA, LUCY; HORNER, DORILANT *following them*]

HAR.    Come, Sparkish, your mistress saw you, and will be angry you go not to her. Besides, I would fain be reconciled to her, which none but you can do, dear friend.

SPARK.    Well, that's a better reason, dear friend. I would not go near her now for hers or my own sake; but I can deny you nothing: for though I have known thee a great while, never go, if I do not love thee as well as a new acquaintance.

HAR.    I am obliged to you indeed, dear friend. I would be well with her, only to be well with thee still; for these ties to wives usually dissolve all ties to friends. I would be contented she should enjoy you a-nights, but I would have you to myself a-days as I have had, dear friend.

SPARK.    And thou shalt enjoy me a-days, dear, dear friend, never stir: and I'll be divorced from her, sooner than from thee. Come along.

HAR. [*aside*]    So, we are hard put to't, when we make our rival our procurer; but neither she nor her brother would let me come near her now. When all's done, a rival is the best cloak to steal to a mistress under, without suspicion; and when we have once got to her as we desire, we throw him off like other cloaks.

[*exit* SPARKISH, *and* HARCOURT *following him*]

*Re-enter* PINCHWIFE, MRS. PINCHWIFE *in man's clothes*

PINCH. [*to* ALITHEA]    Sister, if you will not go, we must leave you.—— [*aside*] The fool her gallant and she will muster up all the young saunterers of this place, and they will leave their dear seamstresses to follow us. What a swarm of cuckolds and cuckold-makers are here!—— Come, let's be gone, Mistress Margery.

MRS. PINCH.    Don't you believe that; I han't half my bellyfull of sights yet.

PINCH.    Then walk this way.

MRS. PINCH.    Lord, what a power of brave signs are here! stay—the Bull's-Head, the Ram's-Head, and the Stag's-Head, dear——

PINCH.    Nay, if every husband's proper sign here were visible, they would be all alike.

MRS. PINCH.    What d'ye mean by that, bud?

PINCH.    'Tis no matter—no matter, bud.

MRS. PINCH.    Pray tell me: nay, I will know.

PINCH.    They would be all Bulls', Stags', and Rams'-heads.

[*exeunt* MR. PINCHWIFE *and* MRS. PINCHWIFE]

*Re-enter* SPARKISH, HARCOURT, ALITHEA, LUCY, *at t'other door*

SPARK.    Come, dear Madam, for my sake you shall be reconciled to him.

ALITH.    For your sake I hate him.

HAR.    That's something too cruel, Madam, to hate me for his sake.

SPARK.    Ay indeed, Madam, too, too cruel to me, to hate my friend for my sake.

ALITH.    I hate him because he is your enemy; and you ought to hate him too, for making love to me, if you love me.

SPARK.    That's a good one! I hate a man for loving you! If he did love you, 'tis but what he can't help; and 'tis your fault, not his, if he admires you. I hate a man for being of my opinion? I'll n'er do't, by the world!

ALITH.    Is it for your honour, or mine, to suffer a man to make love to me, who am to marry you to-morrow?

SPARK.    Is it for your honour, or mine, to have me jealous? That he makes love to you, is a sign you are handsome; and that I am not jealous, is a sign you are virtuous. That I think is for your honour.

ALITH.    But 'tis your honour too I am concerned for.

HAR.    But why, dearest Madam, will you be more concerned for his honour than he is himself? Let his honour alone, for my sake and his. He! he has no honour——

SPARK.    How's that?

HAR.    But what my dear friend can guard himself.

SPARK.    Oh ho—that's right again.

HAR.    Your care of his honour argues his neglect of it, which is no honour to my dear friend here. Therefore once more, let his honour go which way it will, dear Madam.

SPARK.    Ay, ay; were it for my honour to marry a woman whose virtue I suspected, and could not trust her in a friend's hands?

ALITH.    Are you not afraid to lose me?

HAR.    He afraid to lose you, Madam! No, no—you may see how the most estimable and most glorious creature in the world is valued by him. Will you not see it?

SPARK.    Right, honest Frank, I have that noble value for her that I cannot be jealous of her.

ALITH.    You mistake him. He means, you care not for me, nor who has me.

SPARK.    Lord, Madam, I see you are jealous! Will you wrest a poor man's meaning from his words?

ALITH.    You astonish me, Sir, with your want of jealousy.

SPARK.    And you make me giddy, Madam, with your jealousy and fears, and virtue and honour. 'Gad, I see virtue makes a woman as troublesome as a little reading or learning.

ALITH.    Monstrous!

LUCY. [*behind*]    Well, to see what easy husbands these women of quality can meet with! a poor chambermaid can never have such ladylike luck. Besides, he's thrown away upon her. She'll make no use of her fortune, her blessing, none to a gentleman, for a pure cuckold, for it requires good breeding to be a cuckold.

ALITH.    I tell you then plainly, he pursues me to marry me.

SPARK.    Pshaw!

HAR.    Come, Madam, you see you strive in vain to make him jealous of me. My dear friend is the kindest creature in the world to me.

SPARK.    Poor fellow!

HAR.    But his kindness only is not enough for me, without your favour, your good opinion, dear Madam: 'tis that must perfect my happiness. Good gentleman, he believes all I say: would you would do so! Jealous of me! I would not wrong him nor you for the world.

SPARK.    Look you there. Hear him, hear him, and do not walk away so.                                        [ALITHEA *walks carelessly to and fro*]

HAR.    I love you, Madam, so——

SPARK.    How's that? Nay, now you begin to go too far indeed.

HAR.    So much, I confess, I say, I love you, that I would not have you miserable, and cast yourself away upon so unworthy and inconsiderable a thing as what you see here.

[*clapping his hand on his breast, points at* SPARKISH]

SPARK.    No, faith, I believe thou wouldst not: now his meaning is plain; but I knew before thou wouldst not wrong me, nor her.

HAR.    No, no, Heavens forbid the glory of her sex should fall so low, as into the embraces of such a contemptible wretch, the last of mankind—my friend here—I injure him!                    [*embracing* SPARKISH]

ALITH.    Very well.

SPARK.    No, no, dear friend, I knew it.——Madam, you see he will rather wrong himself than me, in giving himself such names.

ALITH.  Do not you understand him yet?

SPARK.  Yes: how modestly he speaks of himself, poor fellow!

ALITH.  Methinks he speaks impudently of yourself, since—before yourself too; insomuch that I can no longer suffer his scurrilous abusiveness to you, no more than his love to me.          [*offers to go*]

SPARK.  Nay, nay, Madam, pray stay—his love to you! Lord, Madam, has he not spoke yet plain enough?

ALITH.  Yes, indeed, I should think so.

SPARK.  Well then, by the world, a man can't speak civilly to a woman now, but presently she says he makes love to her. Nay, Madam, you shall stay, with your pardon, since you have not yet understood him, till he has made an *éclaircissement* of his love to you, that is, what kind of love it is. Answer to thy catechism, friend; do you love my mistress here?

HAR.  Yes, I wish she would not doubt it.

SPARK.  But how do you love her?

HAR.  With all my soul.

ALITH.  I thank him, methinks he speaks plain enough now.

SPARK.  [*to* ALITHEA]  You are out still.——But with what kind of love, Harcourt?

HAR.  With the best and the truest love in the world.

SPARK.  Look you there then, that is with no matrimonial love, I'm sure.

ALITH.  How's that? do you say matrimonial love is not best?

SPARK.  'Gad, I went too far ere I was aware. But speak for thyself, Harcourt, you said you would not wrong me nor her.

HAR.  No, no, Madam, e'en take him for Heaven's sake——

SPARK.  Look you there, Madam.

HAR.  Who should in all justice be yours, he that loves you most.
          [*claps his hand on his breast*]

ALITH.  Look you there, Mr. Sparkish, who's that?

SPARK.  Who should it be?——Go on, Harcourt.

HAR.  Who loves you more than women, titles, or fortune fools.
          [*points at* SPARKISH]

SPARK.  Look you there, he means me still, for he points at me.

ALITH.  Ridiculous!

HAR.  Who can only match your faith and constancy in love.

SPARK.  Ay.

HAR.  Who knows, if it be possible, how to value so much beauty and virtue.

SPARK.  Ay.

HAR.  Whose love can no more be equalled in the world, than that heavenly form of yours.

SPARK.    No.

HAR.    Who could no more suffer a rival than your absence, and yet could no more suspect your virtue than his own constancy in his love to you.

SPARK.    No.

HAR.    Who, in fine, loves you better than his eyes, that first made him love you.

SPARK.    Ay—— Nay, Madam, faith, you shan't go till——

ALITH.    Have a care, lest you make me stay too long.

SPARK.    But till he has saluted you; that I may be assured you are friends, after his honest advice and declaration. Come, pray, Madam, be friends with him.

### Enter MASTER PINCHWIFE, MRS. PINCHWIFE

ALITH.    You must pardon me, Sir, that I am not yet so obedient to you.

PINCH.    What, invite your wife to kiss men? Monstrous! Are you not ashamed? I will never forgive you.

SPARK.    Are you not ashamed that I should have more confidence in the chastity of your family than you have? You must not teach me; I am a man of honour, Sir, though I am frank and free; I am frank, Sir——

PINCH.    Very frank, Sir, to share your wife with your friends.

SPARK.    He is an humble, menial friend, such as reconciles the differences of the marriage bed; you know man and wife do not always agree; I design him for that use, therefore would have him well with my wife.

PINCH.    A menial friend!—you will get a great many menial friends, by showing your wife as you do.

SPARK.    What then? It may be I have a pleasure in't, as I have to show fine clothes at a playhouse, the first day, and count money before poor rogues.

PINCH.    He that shows his wife or money, will be in danger of having them borrowed sometimes.

SPARK.    I love to be envied, and would not marry a wife that I alone could love; loving alone is as dull as eating alone. Is it not a frank age? and I am a frank person; and to tell you the truth, it may be I love to have rivals in a wife; they make her seem to a man still but as a kept mistress; and so good night, for I must to Whitehall.——Madam, I hope you are now reconciled to my friend; and so I wish you a good night, Madam, and sleep if you can: for to-morrow you know I must visit you early with a canonical gentleman. Good night, dear Harcourt.        [*exit* SPARKISH]

HAR.    Madam, I hope you will not refuse my visit to-morrow, if it should be earlier with a canonical gentleman than Mr. Sparkish's.

PINCH.   This gentlewoman is yet under my care, therefore you must yet forbear your freedom with her, Sir.

[*coming between* ALITHEA *and* HARCOURT]

HAR.   Must, Sir?

PINCH.   Yes, Sir, she is my sister.

HAR.   'Tis well she is, Sir—for I must be her servant, Sir.—— Madam——

PINCH.   Come away, Sister, we had been gone, if it had not been for you, and so avoided these lewd rake-hells, who seem to haunt us.

### Enter HORNER, DORILANT *to them*

HORN.   How now, Pinchwife!

PINCH.   Your servant.

HORN.   What! I see a little time in the country makes a man turn wild and unsociable, and only fit to converse with his horses, dogs, and his herds.

PINCH.   I have business, Sir, and must mind it; your business is pleasure; therefore you and I must go different ways.

HORN.   Well, you may go on, but this pretty young gentleman——

[*takes hold of* MRS. PINCHWIFE]

HAR.   The lady——

DOR.   And the maid——

HORN.   Shall stay with us; for I suppose their business is the same with ours, pleasure.

PINCH. [*aside*]   'Sdeath, he knows her, she carries it so sillily! Yet if he does not, I should be more silly to discover it first.

ALITH.   Pray, let us go, Sir.

PINCH.   Come, come——

HORN. [*to* MRS. PINCHWIFE]   Had you not rather stay with us?—— Prithee, Pinchwife, who is this pretty young gentleman?

PINCH.   One to whom I'm a guardian.—[*aside*] I wish I could keep her out of your hands.

HORN.   Who is he? I never saw anything so pretty in all my life.

PINCH.   Pshaw! do not look upon him so much, he's a poor bashful youth; you'll put him out of countenance.——Come away, brother.

[*offers to take her away*]

HORN.   Oh, your brother!

PINCH.   Yes, my wife's brother.——Come, come, she'll stay supper for us.

HORN.   I thought so, for he is very like her I saw you at the play with, whom I told you I was in love with.

MRS. PINCH. [*aside*]   O jeminy! is that he that was in love with me? I am glad on't, I vow, for he's a curious fine gentleman, and I love him already, too.—[to PINCHWIFE] Is this he, bud?

PINCH. [to his Wife]   Come away, come away.

HORN.   Why, what haste are you in? why won't you let me talk with him?

PINCH.   Because you'll debauch him; he's yet young and innocent, and I would not have him debauched for anything in the world.—[aside] How she gazes on him! the devil!

HORN.   Harcourt, Dorilant, look you here, this is the likeness of that dowdy he told us of, his wife; did you ever see a lovelier creature? The rogue has reason to be jealous of his wife, since she is like him, for she would make all that see her in love with her.

HAR.   And, as I remember now, she is as like him here as can be.

DOR.   She is indeed very pretty, if she be like him.

HORN.   Very pretty? a very pretty commendation!—she is a glorious creature, beautiful beyond all things I ever beheld.

PINCH.   So, so.

HAR.   More beautiful than a poet's first mistress of imagination.

HORN.   Or another man's last mistress of flesh and blood.

MRS. PINCH.   Nay, now you jeer, Sir; pray don't jeer me.

PINCH.   Come, come.—[aside] By Heavens, she'll discover herself!

HORN.   I speak of your sister, Sir.

PINCH.   Ay, but saying she was handsome, if like him, made him blush.—[aside] I am upon a rack!

HORN.   Methinks he is so handsome he should not be a man.

PINCH. [aside]   Oh, there 'tis out! he has discovered her! I am not able to suffer any longer.—[to his Wife] Come, come away, I say.

HORN.   Nay, by your leave, Sir, he shall not go yet.—[aside to them] Harcourt, Dorilant, let us torment this jealous rogue a little.

HAR. ⎫
      ⎬ How?
DOR. ⎭

HORN.   I'll show you.

PINCH.   Come, pray let him go, I cannot stay fooling any longer; I tell you his sister stays supper for us.

HORN.   Does she? Come then, we'll all go to sup with he and thee.

PINCH.   No, now I think on't, having stayed so long for us, I warrant she's gone to bed.—[aside] I wish she and I were well out of their hands.——Come, I must rise early to-morrow, come.

HORN.   Well then, if she be gone to bed, I wish her and you a good night. But pray, young gentleman, present my humble service to her.

MRS. PINCH.   Thank you heartily, Sir.

PINCH. [aside]   'Sdeath, she will discover herself yet in spite of me. ——He is something more civil to you, for your kindness to his sister, than I am, it seems.

HORN.   Tell her, dear sweet little gentleman, for all your brother there, that you have revived the love I had for her at first sight in the play-house.

MRS. PINCH.   But did you love her indeed, and indeed?

PINCH. [*aside*]   So, so.——Away, I say.

HORN.   Nay, stay.——Yes, indeed, and indeed, pray do you tell her so, and give her this kiss from me.                                    [*kisses her*]

PINCH. [*aside*]   O Heavens! what do I suffer? Now 'tis too plain he knows her, and yet——

HORN.   And this, and this——                              [*kisses her again*]

MRS. PINCH.   What do you kiss me for? I am no woman.

PINCH. [*aside*]   So, there, 'tis out.—Come, I cannot, nor will stay any longer.

HORN.   Nay, they shall send your lady a kiss too. Here, Harcourt, Dorilant, will you not?                                          [*they kiss her*]

PINCH. [*aside*]   How! do I suffer this? Was I not accusing another just now for this rascally patience, in permitting his wife to be kissed before his face? Ten thousand ulcers gnaw away their lips.——Come, come.

HORN.   Good night, dear little gentleman; Madam, good night; farewell, Pinchwife.——[*apart to* HARCOURT *and* DORILANT] Did not I tell you I would raise his jealous gall?

                          [*exeunt* HORNER, HARCOURT, *and* DORILANT]

PINCH.   So, they are gone at last; stay, let me see first if the coach be at this door.                                                      [*exit*]

### HORNER, HARCOURT, *and* DORILANT *return*

HORN.   What, not gone yet? Will you be sure to do as I desired you, sweet Sir?

MRS. PINCH.   Sweet Sir, but what will you give me then?

HORN.   Anything. Come away into the next walk.

                          [*exit, hauling away* MRS. PINCHWIFE]

ALITH.   Hold! hold! what d'ye do?

LUCY.   Stay, stay, hold——

HAR.   Hold, Madam, hold, let him present him—he'll come presently; nay, I will never let you go till you answer my question.

                  [ALITHEA, LUCY, *struggling with* HARCOURT *and* DORILANT]

LUCY.   For God's sake, Sir, I must follow 'em.

DOR.   No, I have something to present you with too, you shan't follow them.

### PINCHWIFE *returns*

PINCH.   Where?—how—what's become of?—gone!—whither?

LUCY.    He's only gone with the gentleman, who will give him something, an't please your worship.

PINCH.    Something!—give him something, with a pox!—where are they?

ALITH.    In the next walk only, Brother.

PINCH.    Only, only! where, where?

[*exit* PINCHWIFE *and returns presently, then goes out again*]

HAR.    What's the matter with him? Why so much concerned? But, dearest Madam——

ALITH.    Pray let me go, Sir; I have said and suffered enough already.

HAR.    Then you will not look upon, nor pity, my sufferings?

ALITH.    To look upon 'em, when I cannot help 'em, were cruelty, not pity; therefore, I will never see you more.

HAR.    Let me then, Madam, have my privilege of a banished lover, complaining or railing, and giving you but a farewell reason why, if you cannot condescend to marry me, you should not take that wretch, my rival.

ALITH.    He only, not you, since my honour is engaged so far to him, can give me a reason why I should not marry him; but if he be true, and what I think him to me, I must be so to him. Your servant, Sir.

HAR.    Have women only constancy when 'tis a vice, and, like Fortune, only true to fools?

DOR.    Thou shalt not stir, thou robust creature; you see I can deal with you, therefore you should stay the rather, and be kind.

[*to* LUCY, *who struggles to get from him*]

*Enter* PINCHWIFE

PINCH.    Gone, gone, not to be found! quite gone! ten thousand plagues go with 'em! which way went they?

ALITH.    But into t'other walk, Brother.

LUCY.    Their business will be done presently sure, an't please your worship; it can't be long in doing, I'm sure on't.

ALITH.    Are they not there?

PINCH.    No, you know where they are, you infamous wretch, eternal shame of your family, which you do not dishonour enough yourself you think, but you must help her to do it too, thou legion of bawds!

ALITH.    Good Brother——

PINCH.    Damned, damned Sister!

ALITH.    Look you here, she's coming.

*Enter* MRS. PINCHWIFE *in man's clothes, running, with her hat under her arm, full of oranges and dried fruit,* HORNER *following*

MRS. PINCH.   O dear bud, look you here what I have got, see!

PINCH.   [*aside, rubbing his forehead*]   And what I have got here too, which you can't see.

MRS. PINCH.   The fine gentleman has given me better things yet.

PINCH.   Has he so?—[*aside*] Out of breath and coloured!—I must hold yet.

HORN.   I have only given your little brother an orange, Sir.

PINCH.   [*to* HORNER] Thank you, Sir.—[*aside*] You have only squeezed my orange, I suppose, and given it me again; yet I must have a city patience.—[*to his Wife*] Come, come away.

MRS. PINCH.   · Stay, till I have put up my fine things, bud.

### *Enter* SIR JASPER FIDGET

SIR JASP.   O, Master Horner, come, come, the ladies stay for you; your mistress, my wife, wonders you make not more haste to her.

HORN.   I have stayed this half hour for you here, and 'tis your fault I am not now with your wife.

SIR JASP.   But, pray, don't let her know so much; the truth on't is, I was advancing a certain project to his majesty about—I'll tell you.

HORN.   No, let's go, and hear it at your house. Good night, sweet little gentleman; one kiss more, you'll remember me now, I hope.

[*kisses her*]

DOR.   What, Sir Jasper, will you separate friends? He promised to sup with us, and if you take him to your house, you'll be in danger of our company too.

SIR JASP.   Alas! gentlemen, my house is not fit for you; there are none but civil women there, which are not for your turn. He, you know, can bear with the society of civil women now, ha! ha! ha! besides, he's one of my family—he's—he! he! he!

DOR.   What is he?

SIR JASP.   Faith, my eunuch, since you'll have it; he! he! he!

[*Exeunt* SIR JASPER FIDGET *and* HORNER]

DOR.   I rather wish thou wert his or my cuckold. Harcourt, what a good cuckold is lost there for want of a man to make him one! Thee and I cannot have Horner's privilege, who can make use of it.

HAR.   Ay, to poor Horner 'tis like coming to an estate at threescore, when a man can't be the better for't.

PINCH.   Come.

MRS. PINCH.   Presently, bud.

DOR.   Come, let us go too.—[*to* ALITHEA] Madam, your servant.— [*to* LUCY] Good night, strapper.

HAR.   Madam, though you will not let me have a good day or night, I wish you one; but dare not name the other half of my wish.

ALITH.   Good night, Sir, for ever.

MRS. PINCH.   I don't know where to put this here, dear bud, you shall eat it; nay, you shall have part of the fine gentleman's good things, or treat, as you call it, when we come home.

PINCH.   Indeed, I deserve it, since I furnished the best part of it.

[strikes away the orange]

> The gallant treats presents, and gives the ball;
> But 'tis the absent cuckold pays for all.

# ACT IV

## SCENE I

*In* PINCHWIFE'S *House in the morning*

LUCY, ALITHEA *dressed in new clothes*

LUCY. Well, Madam,—now have I dressed you, and set you out with so many ornaments, and spent upon you ounces of essence and pulvillio; and all this for no other purpose but as people adorn and perfume a corpse for a stinking second-hand grave: such, or as bad, I think Master Sparkish's bed.

ALITH. Hold your peace.

LUCY. Nay, Madam, I will ask you the reason why you would banish poor Master Harcourt for ever from your sight; how could you be so hard-hearted?

ALITH. 'Twas because I was not hard-hearted.

LUCY. No, no; 'twas stark love and kindness, I warrant.

ALITH. It was so; I would see him no more because I love him.

LUCY. Hey day, a very pretty reason!

ALITH. You do not understand me.

LUCY. I wish you may yourself.

ALITH. I was engaged to marry, you see, another man, whom my justice will not suffer me to deceive or injure.

LUCY. Can there be a greater cheat or wrong done to a man than to give him your person without your heart? I should make a conscience of it.

ALITH. I'll retrieve it for him after I am married a while.

LUCY. The woman that marries to love better, will be as much mistaken as the wencher that marries to live better. No, Madam, marrying to increase love is like gaming to become rich; alas! you only lose what little stock you had before.

ALITH. I find by your rhetoric you have been bribed to betray me.

LUCY. Only by his merit, that has bribed your heart, you see, against your word and rigid honour. But what a devil is this honour! 'tis sure a

46

disease in the head, like the megrim or falling-sickness, that always hurries people away to do themselves mischief. Men lose their lives by it; women, what's dearer to 'em, their love, the life of life.

ALITH.    Come, pray talk you no more of honour, nor Master Harcourt; I wish the other would come to secure my fidelity to him and his right in me.

LUCY.    You will marry him then?

ALITH.    Certainly; I have given him already my word, and will my hand too, to make it good, when he comes.

LUCY.    Well, I wish I may never stick pin more, if he be not an arrant natural to t'other fine gentleman.

ALITH.    I own he wants the wit of Harcourt, which I will dispense withal for another want he has, which is want of jealousy, which men of wit seldom want.

LUCY.    Lord, Madam, what should you do with a fool to your husband? You intend to be honest, don't you? then that husbandly virtue, credulity, is thrown away upon you.

ALITH.    He only that could suspect my virtue should have cause to do it; 'tis Sparkish's confidence in my truth that obliges me to be so faithful to him.

LUCY.    You are not sure his opinion may last.

ALITH.    I am satisfied 'tis impossible for him to be jealous after the proofs I have had of him. Jealousy in a husband—Heaven defend me from it! it begets a thousand plagues to a poor woman, the loss of her honour, her quiet, and her——

LUCY.    And her pleasure.

ALITH.    What d'ye mean, impertinent?

LUCY.    Liberty is a great pleasure, Madam.

ALITH.    I say, loss of her honour, her quiet, nay, her life sometimes; and what's as bad almost, the loss of this town; that is, she is sent into the country, which is the last ill-usage of a husband to a wife, I think.

LUCY [aside]    Oh, does the wind lie there?—— Then of necessity, Madam, you think a man must carry his wife into the country, if he be wise. The country is as terrible, I find, to our young English ladies, as a monastery to those abroad; and, on my virginity, I think they would rather marry a London jailer than a high sheriff of a county, since neither can stir from his employment. Formerly women of wit married fools for a great estate, a fine seat, or the like; but now 'tis for a pretty seat only in Lincoln's Inn Fields, St. James's Fields, or the Pall Mall.

*Enter to them* SPARKISH, *and* HARCOURT, *dressed like a Parson*

SPARK.    Madam, your humble servant, a happy day to you, and to us all.

HAR.    Amen.

ALITH.    Who have we here?

SPARK.    My chaplain, faith—— O Madam, poor Harcourt remembers his humble service to you; and, in obedience to your last commands, refrains coming into your sight.

ALITH.    Is not that he?

SPARK.    No, fy, no; but to show that he ne'er intended to hinder our match, has sent his brother here to join our hands. When I get me a wife, I must get her a chaplain, according to the custom; that is his brother, and my chaplain.

ALITH.    His brother!

LUCY. [*aside*]    And your chaplain, to preach in your pulpit then——

ALITH.    His brother!

SPARK.    Nay, I knew you would not believe it.—— I told you, Sir, she would take you for your brother Frank.

ALITH.    Believe it!

LUCY. [*aside*]    His brother! ha! ha! he! he has a trick left still, it seems.

SPARK.    Come, my dearest, pray let us go to church before the canonical hour is past.

ALITH.    For shame, you are abused still.

SPARK.    By the world, 'tis strange now you are so incredulous.

ALITH.    'Tis strange you are so credulous.

SPARK.    Dearest of my life, hear me. I tell you this is Ned Harcourt of Cambridge, by the world; you see he has a sneaking college look. 'Tis true he's something like his brother Frank; and they differ from each other no more than in their age, for they were twins.

LUCY.    Ha! ha! he!

ALITH.    Your servant, Sir; I cannot be so deceived, though you are. But come, let's hear, how do you know what you affirm so confidently?

SPARK.    Why, I'll tell you all. Frank Harcourt coming to me this morning to wish me joy, and present his service to you, I asked him if he could help me to a parson. Whereupon he told me he had a brother in town who was in orders; and he went straight away, and sent him, you see there, to me.

ALITH.    Yes, Frank goes and puts on a black coat, then tells you he is Ned; that's all you have for't.

SPARK.    Pshaw! pshaw! I tell you, by the same token, the midwife put her garter about Frank's neck, to know 'em asunder, they were so like.

ALITH.    Frank tells you this too?

SPARK.    Ay, and Ned there too: nay, they are both in a story.

ALITH.    So, so; very foolish.

SPARK.    Lord, if you won't believe one, you had best try him by your chambermaid there; for chambermaids must needs know chaplains from other men, they are so used to 'em.

LUCY.    Let's see: nay, I'll be sworn he has the canonical smirk, and the filthy clammy palm of a chaplain.

ALITH.    Well, most reverend Doctor, pray let us make an end of this fooling.

HAR.    With all my soul, divine heavenly creature, when you please.

ALITH.    He speaks like a chaplain indeed.

SPARK.    Why, was there not soul, divine, heavenly, in what he said?

ALITH.    Once more, most impertinent black coat, cease your persecution, and let us have a conclusion of this ridiculous love.

HAR. [aside]    I had forgot; I must suit my style to my coat, or I wear it in vain.

ALITH.    I have no more patience left; let us make once an end of this troublesome love, I say.

HAR.    So be it, seraphic lady, when your honour shall think it meet and convenient so to do.

SPARK.    'Gad, I'm sure none but a chaplain could speak so, I think.

ALITH.    Let me tell you, Sir, this dull trick will not serve your turn; though you delay our marriage, you shall not hinder it.

HAR.    Far be it from me, munificent patroness, to delay your marriage; I desire nothing more than to marry you presently, which I might do, if you yourself would; for my noble, good-natured, and thrice generous patron here would not hinder it.

SPARK.    No, poor man, not I, faith.

HAR.    And now, Madam, let me tell you plainly nobody else shall marry you, by Heavens! I'll die first, for I'm sure I should die after it.

LUCY.    How his love has made him forget his function, as I have seen it in real parsons!

ALITH.    That was spoken like a chaplain too? Now you understand him, I hope.

SPARK.    Poor man, he takes it heinously to be refused; I can't blame him, 'tis putting an indignity upon him, not to be suffered; but you'll pardon me, Madam, it shan't be; he shall marry us; come away, pray, Madam.

LUCY.    Ha! ha! he! more ado! 'tis late.

ALITH.    Invincible stupidity! I tell you, he would marry me as your rival, not as your chaplain.

SPARK.    Come, come, Madam.                              [pulling her away]

LUCY.    I pray, Madam, do not refuse this reverend divine the honour and satisfaction of marrying you; for I dare say he has set his heart upon't, good Doctor.

ALITH.    What can you hope or design by this?

HAR. [aside]    I could answer her, a reprieve for a day only, often revokes a hasty doom. At worst, if she will not take mercy on me, and let me marry her, I have at least the lover's second pleasure, hindering my rival's enjoyment, though but for a time.

SPARK.    Come, Madam, 'tis e'en twelve o'clock, and my mother charged me never to be married out of the canonical hours. Come, come; Lord, here's such a deal of modesty, I warrant, the first day.

LUCY.    Yes, an't please your worship, married women show all their modesty the first day, because married men show all their love the first day.                     [*exeunt* SPARKISH, ALITHEA, HARCOURT, *and* LUCY]

## SCENE II

*The Scene changes to a Bedchamber, where appear* PINCHWIFE *and* MRS. PINCHWIFE

PINCH.    Come, tell me, I say.

MRS. PINCH.    Lord! han't I told it a hundred times over?

PINCH. [*aside*]    I would try, if in the repetition of the ungrateful tale, I could find her altering it in the least circumstance; for if her story be false, she is so too.——— Come, how was't, baggage?

MRS. PINCH.    Lord, what pleasure you take to hear it, sure!

PINCH.    No, you take more in telling it I find; but speak, how was't?

MRS. PINCH.    He carried me up into the house next to the Exchange.

PINCH.    So, and you two were only in the room!

MRS. PINCH.    Yes, for he sent away a youth that was there, for some dried fruit, and China oranges.

PINCH.    Did he so? Damn him for it—and for——

MRS. PINCH.    But presently came up the gentlewoman of the house.

PINCH.    Oh, 'twas well she did; but what did he do whilst the fruit came?

MRS. PINCH.    He kissed me an hundred times, and told me he fancied he kissed my fine sister, meaning me, you know, whom he said he loved with all his soul, and bid me be sure to tell her so, and to desire her to be at her window, by eleven of the clock this morning, and he would walk under it at that time.

PINCH. [*aside*]    And he was as good as his word, very punctual; a pox reward him for't.

MRS. PINCH.    Well, and he said if you were not within, he would come up to her, meaning me, you know, bud, still.

PINCH. [*aside*]    So—he knew her certainly; but for this confession, I am obliged to her simplicity.——But what, you stood very still when he kissed you?

MRS. PINCH.    Yes, I warrant you; would you have had me discover myself?

PINCH.   But you told me he did some beastliness to you, as you call it; what was't?

MRS. PINCH.   Why, he put——

PINCH.   What?

MRS. PINCH.   Why, he put the tip of his tongue between my lips, and so mousled me—and I said, I'd bite it.

PINCH.   An eternal canker seize it, for a dog!

MRS. PINCH.   Nay, you need not be so angry with him neither, for to say truth, he has the sweetest breath I ever knew.

PINCH.   The devil! you were satisfied with it then, and would do it again?

MRS. PINCH.   Not unless he should force me.

PINCH.   Force you, changeling! I tell you, no woman can be forced.

MRS. PINCH.   Yes, but she may sure, by such a one as he, for he's a proper, goodly, strong man; 'tis hard, let me tell you, to resist him.

PINCH. [aside]   So, 'tis plain she loves him, yet she has not love enough to make her conceal it from me; but the sight of him will increase her aversion for me and love for him; and that love instruct her how to deceive me and satisfy him, all idiot as she is. Love! 'twas he gave women first their craft, their art of deluding. Out of Nature's hands they came plain, open, silly, and fit for slaves, as she and Heaven intended 'em; but damned Love—well—I must strangle that little monster whilst I can deal with him.—— Go fetch pen, ink, and paper out of the next room.

MRS. PINCH.   Yes, bud.                                        [exit]

PINCH.   Why should women have more invention in love than men? It can only be, because they have more desires, more soliciting passions, more lust, and more of the devil.

MRS. PINCHWIFE returns

Come, minx, sit down and write.

MRS. PINCH.   Ay, dear bud, but I can't do't very well.

PINCH.   I wish you could not at all.

MRS. PINCH.   But what should I write for?

PINCH.   I'll have you write a letter to your lover.

MRS. PINCH.   O Lord, to the fine gentleman a letter!

PINCH.   Yes, to the fine gentleman.

MRS. PINCH.   Lord, you do but jeer: sure you jest.

PINCH.   I am not so merry: come, write as I bid you.

MRS. PINCH.   What, do you think I am a fool?

PINCH. [aside]   She's afraid I would not dictate any love to him, therefore she's unwilling.—But you had best begin.

MRS. PINCH.   Indeed, and indeed, but I won't, so I won't.

PINCH.   Why?

MRS. PINCH.    Because he's in town; you may send for him if you will.

PINCH.    Very well, you would have him brought to you; is it come to this? I say, take the pen and write, or you'll provoke me.

MRS. PINCH.    Lord, what d'ye make a fool of me for? Don't I know that letters are never writ but from the country to London, and from London into the country? Now he's in town, and I am in town too; therefore I can't write to him, you know.

PINCH. [aside]    So, I am glad it is no worse; she is innocent enough yet.— Yes, you may, when your husband bids you, write letters to people that are in town.

MRS. PINCH.    Oh, may I so? then I'm satisfied.

PINCH.    Come, begin [dictates]—"Sir"——

MRS. PINCH.    Shan't I say, "Dear Sir?" You know one says always something more than bare "Sir."

PINCH.    Write as I bid you, or I will write whore with this penknife in your face.

MRS. PINCH.    Nay, good bud [she writes]—"Sir"——

PINCH.    "Though I suffered last night your nauseous, loathed kisses and embraces"—— Write!

MRS. PINCH.    Nay, why should I say so? You know I told you he had a sweet breath.

PINCH.    Write!

MRS. PINCH.    Let me but put out "loathed."

PINCH.    Write, I say!

MRS. PINCH.    Well then.                                                      [writes]

PINCH.    Let's see, what have you writ?—[takes the paper and reads] "Though I suffered last night your kisses and embraces"—— Thou impudent creature! where is "nauseous" and "loathed"?

MRS. PINCH.    I can't abide to write such filthy words.

PINCH.    Once more write as I'd have you, and question it not, or I will spoil thy writing with this. I will stab out those eyes that cause my mischief.                                                      [holds up the penknife]

MRS. PINCH.    O Lord! I will.

PINCH.    So—so—let's see now.—[reads] "Though I suffered last night your nauseous, loathed kisses and embraces"—go on—"yet I would not have you presume that you shall ever repeat them"—so——    [she writes]

MRS. PINCH.    I have writ it.

PINCH.    On, then—"I then concealed myself from your knowledge, to avoid your insolencies."——                                    [she writes]

MRS. PINCH.    So——

PINCH.    "The same reason, now I am out of your hands"——
                                                                    [she writes]

MRS. PINCH.    So——

PINCH.  "Makes me own to you my unfortunate, though innocent frolic, of being in man's clothes"——                              [*she writes*]

MRS. PINCH.  So——

PINCH.  "That you may for evermore cease to pursue her, who hates and detests you"——                                          [*she writes on*]

MRS. PINCH.  So-h——                                            [*sighs*]

PINCH.  What, do you sigh?—"detests you—as much as she loves her husband and her honour."

MRS. PINCH.  I vow, husband, he'll ne'er believe I should write such a letter.

PINCH.  What, he'd expect a kinder from you? Come, now your name only.

MRS. PINCH.  What, shan't I say "Your most faithful humble servant till death?"

PINCH.  No, tormenting fiend!—[*aside*] Her style, I find, would be very soft.—— Come, wrap it up now, whilst I go fetch wax and a candle; and write on the backside, "For Mr. Horner."        [*exit* PINCHWIFE]

MRS. PINCH.  "For Mr. Horner."—— So, I am glad he has told me his name. Dear Mr. Horner! But why should I send thee such a letter that will vex thee, and make thee angry with me?—— Well, I will not send it.—— Ay, but then my husband will kill me—for I see plainly he won't let me love Mr. Horner—but what care I for my husband? I won't, so I won't, send poor Mr. Horner such a letter—— But then my husband—but oh, what if I writ at bottom my husband made me write it?—— Ay, but then my husband would see't—Can one have no shift? Ah, a London woman would have had a hundred presently. Stay—what if I should write a letter, and wrap it up like this, and write upon't too? Ay, but then my husband would see't—I don't know what to do.—But yet evads I'll try, so I will—for I will not send this letter to poor Mr. Horner, come what will on't.

"Dear, sweet Mr. Horner"—[*she writes and repeats what she hath writ*]—so—"my husband would have me send you a base, rude, unmannerly letter; but I won't"—so—"and would have me forbid you loving me; but I won't"—so—"and would have me say to you, I hate you, poor Mr. Horner; but I won't tell a lie for him"—there—"for I'm sure if you and I were in the country at cards together"—so—"I could not help treading on your toe under the table"—so—"or rubbing knees with you, and staring in your face, till you saw me"—very well—"and then looking down, and blushing for an hour together"—so—"but I must make haste before my husband come: and now he has taught me to write letters, you shall have longer ones from me, who am, dear, dear, poor, dear Mr. Horner, your most humble friend, and servant to command till death,—Margery Pinchwife."

Stay, I must give him a hint at bottom——so——now wrap it up just like t'other——so——now write "For Mr. Horner"——But oh now, what shall I do with it? for here comes my husband.

*Enter* PINCHWIFE

PINCH. [*aside*]   I have been detained by a sparkish coxcomb, who pretended a visit to me; but I fear 'twas to my wife—— What, have you done?

MRS. PINCH.   Ay, ay, bud, just now.

PINCH.   Let's see't: what d'ye tremble for? what, you would not have it go?

MRS. PINCH.   Here——[*aside*] No, I must not give him that: so I had been served if I had given him this.      [*he opens and reads the first letter*]

PINCH.   Come, where's the wax and seal?

MRS. PINCH. [*aside*]   Lord, what shall I do now? Nay, then I have it—— Pray let me see't. Lord, you think me so arrant a fool I cannot seal a letter; I will do't, so I will.      [*snatches the letter from him, changes it for the other, seals it, and delivers it to him*]

PINCH.   Nay, I believe you will learn that, and other things too, which I would not have you.

MRS. PINCH.   So, han't I done it curiously?—[*aside*] I think I have; there's my letter going to Mr. Horner, since he'll needs have me send letters to folks.

PINCH.   'Tis very well; but I warrant, you would not have it go now?

MRS. PINCH.   Yes, indeed, but I would, bud, now.

PINCH.   Well, you are a good girl then. Come, let me lock you up in your chamber till I come back; and be sure you come not within three strides of the window when I am gone, for I have a spy in the street.——[*exit* MRS. PINCHWIFE, PINCHWIFE *locks the door*] At least, 'tis fit she think so. If we do not cheat women, they'll cheat us, and fraud may be justly used with secret enemies, of which a wife is the most dangerous; and he that has a handsome one to keep, and a frontier town, must provide against treachery, rather than open force. Now I have secured all within, I'll deal with the foe without, with false intelligence.

[*holds up the letter; exit* PINCHWIFE]

## SCENE III

*The Scene changes to* HORNER'S *Lodging*

QUACK *and* HORNER

QUACK.   Well, Sir, how fadges the new design? Have you not the luck of all your brother projectors, to deceive only yourself at last?

HORN.    No, good domine Doctor, I deceive you, it seems, and others too; for the grave matrons, and old, rigid husbands think me as unfit for love as they are; but their wives, sisters, and daughters know, some of 'em, better things already.

QUACK.    Already!

HORN.    Already, I say. Last night I was drunk with half-a-dozen of your civil persons, as you call 'em, and people of honour, and so was made free of their society and dressing-rooms for ever hereafter; and am already come to the privileges of sleeping upon their pallets, warming smocks, tying shoes and garters, and the like, Doctor, already, already, Doctor.

QUACK.    You have made good use of your time, Sir.

HORN.    I tell thee, I am now no more interruption to 'em when they sing, or talk, bawdy, than a little squab French page who speaks no English.

QUACK.    But do civil persons and women of honour drink, and sing bawdy songs?

HORN.    Oh, amongst friends, amongst friends. For your bigots in honour are just like those in religion; they fear the eye of the world more than the eye of Heaven, and think there is no virtue but railing at vice, and no sin but giving scandal. They rail at a poor little kept player, and keep themselves some young modest pulpit comedian to be privy to their sins in their closets, not to tell 'em of them in their chapels.

QUACK.    Nay, the truth on't is priests, amongst the women now, have quite got the better of us lay-confessors, physicians.

HORN.    And they are rather their patients; but——

*Enter* MY LADY FIDGET, *looking about her*

Now we talk of women of honour, here comes one. Step behind the screen there, and but observe if I have not particular privileges with the women of reputation already, Doctor, already.          [QUACK *retires*]

LADY FID.    Well, Horner, am not I a woman of honour? You see, I'm as good as my word.

HORN.    And you shall see, Madam, I'll not behindhand with you in honour; and I'll be as good as my word too, if you please but to withdraw into the next room.

LADY FID.    But first, my dear Sir, you must promise to have a care of my dear honour.

HORN.    If you talk a word more of your honour, you'll make me incapable to wrong it. To talk of honour in the mysteries of love, is like talking of Heaven or the Deity in an operation of witchcraft just when you are employing the devil: it makes the charm impotent.

LADY FID.    Nay, fy! let us not be smutty. But you talk of mysteries and bewitching to me; I don't understand you.

HORN.    I tell you, Madam, the word money in a mistress's mouth, at such a nick of time, is not a more disheartening sound to a younger brother, than that of honour to an eager lover like myself.

LADY FID.    But you can't blame a lady of my reputation to be chary.

HORN.    Chary! I have been chary of it already, by the report I have caused of myself.

LADY FID.    Ay, but if you should ever let other women know that dear secret, it would come out. Nay, you must have a great care of your conduct; for my acquaintance are so censorious (oh, 'tis a wicked, censorious world, Mr. Horner!), I say, are so censorious and detracting that perhaps they'll talk to the prejudice of my honour, though you should not let them know the dear secret.

HORN.    Nay, Madam, rather than they shall prejudice your honour, I'll prejudice theirs; and, to serve you, I'll lie with 'em all, make the secret their own, and then they'll keep it. I am a Machiavel in love, Madam.

LADY FID.    Oh, no, Sir, not that way.

HORN.    Nay, the devil take me, if censorious women are to be silenced any other way.

LADY FID.    A secret is better kept, I hope, by a single person than a multitude; therefore pray do not trust anybody else with it, dear, dear Mr. Horner.                                                  [*embracing him*]

### *Enter* SIR JASPER FIDGET

SIR JASP.    How now!

LADY FID. [*aside*]    Oh my husband!—prevented—and what's almost as bad, found with my arms about another man—that will appear too much—what shall I say?—— Sir Jasper, come hither: I am trying if Mr. Horner were ticklish, and he's as ticklish as can be. I love to torment the confounded toad; let you and I tickle him.

SIR JASP.    No, your ladyship will tickle him better without me, I suppose. But is this your buying china? I thought you had been at the china-house.

HORN. [*aside*]    China-house! that's my cue, I must take it.—— A pox! can't you keep your impertinent wives at home? Some men are troubled with the husbands, but I with the wives; but I'd have you to know, since I cannot be your journeyman by night, I will not be your drudge by day, to squire your wife about, and be your man of straw or scarecrow only to pies and jays, that would be nibbling at your forbidden fruit; I shall be shortly the hackney gentleman-usher of the town.

SIR JASP. [*aside*]    He! he! he! poor fellow, he's in the right on't, faith. To squire women about for other folks is as ungrateful an employment, as to tell money for other folks.—— He! he! he! be'n't angry, Horner.

LADY FID.    No, 'tis I have more reason to be angry, who am left by you to go abroad indecently alone; or, what is more indecent, to pin myself upon such ill-bred people of your acquaintance as this is.

SIR JASP.    Nay, prithee, what has he done?

LADY FID.    Nay, he has done nothing.

SIR JASP.    But what d'ye take ill, if he has done nothing?

LADY FID.    Ha! ha! ha! faith, I can't but laugh, however; why, d'ye think the unmannerly toad would come down to me to the coach? I was fain to come up to fetch him, or go without him, which I was resolved not to do; for he knows china very well, and has himself very good, but will not let me see it lest I should beg some; but I will find it out, and have what I came for yet.

HORN.    [apart to LADY FIDGET]    Lock the door, Madam.—[exit LADY FIDGET, and locks the door followed by HORNER to the door]—— So, she has got into my chamber and locked me out. Oh the impertinency of womankind! Well, Sir Jasper, plain-dealing is a jewel; if ever you suffer your wife to trouble me again here she shall carry you home a pair of horns; by my lord mayor she shall; though I cannot furnish you myself, you are sure, yet I'll find a way.

SIR JASP.    Ha! ha! he!—[aside] At my first coming in, and finding her arms about him, tickling him it seems, I was half jealous, but now I see my folly.—— He! he! he! poor Horner.

HORN.    Nay, though you laugh now, 'twill be my turn ere long. Oh, women, more impertinent, more cunning, and more mischievous than their monkeys, and to me almost as ugly!—Now is she throwing my things about and rifling all I have; but I'll get in to her the back way, and so rifle her for it.

SIR JASP.    Ha! ha! ha! poor angry Horner.

HORN.    Stay here a little, I'll ferret her out to you presently, I warrant.                                                        [exit at t'other door]

[SIR JASPER calls through the door to his Wife; she answers from within]

SIR JASP.    Wife! my Lady Fidget! wife! he is coming in to you the back way.

LADY FID.    Let him come, and welcome, which way he will.

SIR JASP.    He'll catch you, and use you roughly, and be too strong for you.

LADY FID.    Don't you trouble yourself, let him if he can.

QUACK.    [behind]    This indeed I could not have believed from him, nor any but my own eyes.

### Enter MRS. SQUEAMISH

MRS. SQUEAM.    Where's this woman-hater, this toad, this ugly, greasy, dirty sloven?

SIR JASP. [*aside*]   So, the women all will have him ugly: methinks he is a comely person, but his wants make his form contemptible to 'em; and 'tis e'en as my wife said yesterday, talking of him, that a proper handsome eunuch was as ridiculous a thing as a gigantic coward.

MRS. SQUEAM.   Sir Jasper, your servant: where is the odious beast?

SIR JASP.   He's within in his chamber, with my wife; she's playing the wag with him.

MRS. SQUEAM.   Is she so? and he's a clownish beast, he'll give her no quarter, he'll play the wag with her again, let me tell you: come, let's go help her.—What, the door's locked?

SIR JASP.   Ay, my wife locked it.

MRS. SQUEAM.   Did she so? Let's break it open then.

SIR JASP.   No, no; he'll do her no hurt.

MRS. SQUEAM.   No.—[*aside*] But is there no other way to get in to 'em? Whither goes this? I will disturb 'em.

[*exit* MRS. SQUEAMISH *at another door*]

#### Enter OLD LADY SQUEAMISH

LADY SQUEAM.   Where is this harlotry, this impudent baggage, this rambling tomrigg? O Sir Jasper, I'm glad to see you here; did you not see my vile grandchild come in hither just now?

SIR JASP.   Yes.

LADY SQUEAM.   Ay, but where is she then? where is she? Lord, Sir Jasper, I have e'en rattled myself to pieces in pursuit of her: but can you tell what she makes here? They say below, no woman lodges here.

SIR JASP.   No.

LADY SQUEAM.   No! what does she here then? Say, if it be not a woman's lodging, what makes she here? But are you sure no woman lodges here?

SIR JASP.   No, nor no man neither; this is Mr. Horner's lodging.

LADY SQUEAM.   Is it so, are you sure?

SIR JASP.   Yes, yes.

LADY SQUEAM.   So; then there's no hurt in't, I hope. But where is he?

SIR JASP.   He's in the next room with my wife.

LADY SQUEAM.   Nay, if you trust him with your wife, I may with my Biddy. They say, he's a merry harmless man now, e'en as harmless a man as ever came out of Italy with a good voice, and as pretty, harmless company for a lady as a snake without his teeth.

SIR JASP.   Ay, ay, poor man.

#### Enter MRS. SQUEAMISH

MRS. SQUEAM.   I can't find 'em.—— Oh, are you here, Grandmother? I followed, you must know, my Lady Fidget hither; 'tis the prettiest lodging, and I have been staring on the prettiest pictures——

*Enter* LADY FIDGET *with a piece of china in her hand, and* HORNER *following*

LADY FID.    And I have been toiling and moiling for the prettiest piece of china, my dear.

HORN.    Nay, she has been too hard for me, do what I could.

MRS. SQUEAM.    O Lord, I'll have some china too. Good Mr. Horner, don't think to give other people china, and me none; come in with me too.

HORN.    Upon my honour, I have none left now.

MRS. SQUEAM.    Nay, nay, I have known you deny your china before now, but you shan't put me off so. Come.

HORN.    This lady had the last there.

LADY FID.    Yes, indeed, Madam, to my certain knowledge, he has no more left.

MRS. SQUEAM.    Oh, but it may be he may have some you could not find.

LADY FID.    What, d'ye think if he had had any left, I would not have had it too? for we women of quality never think we have china enough.

HORN.    Do not take it ill, I cannot make china for you all, but I will have a roll-waggon for you too, another time.

MRS. SQUEAM.    Thank you, dear toad.

LADY FID. [*aside to* HORNER]    What do you mean by that promise?

HORN. [*aside to* LADY FIDGET]    Alas, she has an innocent, literal understanding.

LADY SQUEAM.    Poor Mr. Horner! he has enough to do to please you all, I see.

HORN.    Ay, Madam, you see how they use me.

LADY SQUEAM.    Poor gentleman, I pity you.

HORN.    I thank you, Madam: I could never find pity but from such reverend ladies as you are; the young ones will never spare a man.

MRS. SQUEAM.    Come, come, beast, and go dine with us; for we shall want a man at ombre after dinner.

HORN.    That's all their use of me, Madam, you see.

MRS. SQUEAM.    Come, sloven, I'll lead you, to be sure of you.

[*pulls him by the cravat*]

LADY SQUEAM.    Alas, poor man, how she tugs him! Kiss, kiss her; that's the way to make such nice women quiet.

HORN.    No, Madam, that remedy is worse than the torment; they know I dare suffer anything rather than do it.

LADY SQUEAM.    Prithee kiss her, and I'll give you her picture in little, that you admired so last night; prithee do.

HORN.    Well, nothing but that could bribe me: I love a woman only in effigy and good painting, as much as I hate them. I'll do't, for I could adore the devil well painted.                    [*kisses* MRS. SQUEAMISH]

MRS. SQUEAM.    Foh, you filthy toad! nay, now I've done jesting.

LADY SQUEAM.    Ha! ha! ha! I told you so.

MRS. SQUEAM.    Foh! a kiss of his——

SIR JASP.    Has no more hurt in't than one of my spaniel's.

MRS. SQUEAM.    Nor no more good neither.

QUACK. [*behind*]    I will now believe anything he tells me.

*Enter* PINCHWIFE

LADY FID.    O Lord, here's a man! Sir Jasper, my mask, my mask! I would not be seen here for the world.

SIR JASP.    What, not when I am with you?

LADY FID.    No, no, my honour—let's be gone.

MRS. SQUEAM.    O Grandmother, let us be gone; make haste, make haste, I know not how he may censure us.

LADY FID.    Be found in the lodging of anything like a man!—Away.

[*exeunt* SIR JASPER FIDGET, LADY FIDGET,
OLD LADY SQUEAMISH, MRS. SQUEAMISH]

QUACK. [*behind*]    What's here? another cuckold? he looks like one, and none else sure have any business with him.

HORN.    Well, what brings my dear friend hither?

PINCH.    Your impertinency.

HORN.    My impertinency!—why, you gentlemen that have got handsome wives think you have a privilege of saying anything to your friends, and are as brutish as if you were our creditors.

PINCH.    No, Sir, I'll ne'er trust you any way.

HORN.    But why not, dear Jack? Why diffide in me thou know'st so well?

PINCH.    Because I do know you so well.

HORN.    Han't I been always thy friend, honest Jack, always ready to serve thee, in love or battle, before thou wert married, and am so still?

PINCH.    I believe so; you would be my second now, indeed.

HORN.    Well then, dear Jack, why so unkind, so grum, so strange to me? Come, prithee kiss me, dear rogue: gad, I was always, I say, and am still as much thy servant as——

PINCH.    As I am yours, Sir. What, you would send a kiss to my wife, is that it?

HORN.    So, there 'tis—a man can't show his friendship to a married man, but presently he talks of his wife to you. Prithee, let thy wife alone, and let thee and I be all one, as we were wont. What, thou art as shy of my kindness as a Lombard Street alderman of a courtier's civility at Locket's!

PINCH.    But you are overkind to me, as kind as if I were your cuckold already; yet I must confess you ought to be kind and civil to me, since
I am so kind, so civil to you, as to bring you this: look you there, Sir.

*[delivers him a letter]*

HORN.    What is't?

PINCH.    Only a love letter, Sir.

HORN.    From whom?—how! this is from your wife—hum—and
hum——                                                     *[reads]*

PINCH.    Even from my wife, Sir: am I not wondrous kind and civil to
you now too?—*[aside]* But you'll not think her so.

HORN. *[aside]*   Ha! is this a trick of his or hers?

PINCH.    The gentleman's surprised I find.—What, you expected a
kinder letter?

HORN.    No faith, not I, how could I?

PINCH.    Yes, yes, I'm sure you did. A man so well made as you are
must needs be disappointed, if the women declare not their passion at
first sight or opportunity.

HORN. *[aside]*   But what should this mean? Stay, the postscript.—
*[reads aside]* "Be sure you love me, whatsoever my husband says to the
contrary, and let him not see this, lest he should come home and pinch
me, or kill my squirrel."—It seems he knows not what the letter contains.

PINCH.    Come, ne'er wonder at it so much.

HORN.    Faith, I can't help it.

PINCH.    Now, I think I have deserved your infinite friendship and
kindness, and have showed myself sufficiently an obliging kind friend and
husband; am I not so, to bring a letter from my wife to her gallant?

HORN.    Ay, the devil take me, art thou, the most obliging, kind friend
and husband in the world, ha! ha!

PINCH.    Well, you may be merry, Sir; but in short I must tell you, Sir,
my honour will suffer no jesting.

HORN.    What dost thou mean?

PINCH.    Does the letter want a comment? Then, know, Sir, though I
have been so civil a husband as to bring you a letter from my wife, to let
you kiss and court her to my face, I will not be a cuckold, Sir, I will not.

HORN.    Thou art mad with jealousy. I never saw thy wife in my life
but at the play yesterday, and I know not if it were she or no. I court her,
kiss her!

PINCH.    I will not be a cuckold, I say; there will be danger in making
me a cuckold.

HORN.    Why, wert thou not well cured of thy last clap?

PINCH.    I wear a sword.

HORN.    It should be taken from thee, lest thou shouldst do thyself a
mischief with it; thou art mad, man.

PINCH.   As mad as I am, and as merry as you are, I must have more reason from you ere we part. I say again, though you kissed and courted last night my wife in man's clothes, as she confesses in her letter——

HORN. [*aside*]   Ha!

PINCH.   Both she and I say you must not design it again, for you have mistaken your woman, as you have done your man.

HORN. [*aside*]   Oh—I understand something now—— Was that thy wife! Why wouldst thou not tell me 'twas she? Faith, my freedom with her was your fault, not mine.

PINCH. [*aside*]   Faith, so 'twas.

HORN.   Fy! I'd never do't to a woman before her husband's face, sure.

PINCH.   But I had rather you should do't to my wife before my face, than behind my back; and that you shall never do.

HORN.   No—you will hinder me.

PINCH.   If I would not hinder you, you see by her letter she would.

HORN.   Well, I must e'en acquiesce then, and be contented with what she writes.

PINCH.   I'll assure you 'twas voluntarily writ; I had no hand in't, you may believe me.

HORN.   I do believe thee, faith.

PINCH.   And believe her too, for she's an innocent creature, has no dissembling in her: and so fare you well, Sir.

HORN.   Pray, however, present my humble service to her, and tell her I will obey her letter to a tittle, and fulfil her desires, be what they will, or with what difficulty soever I do't; and you shall be no more jealous of me, I warrant her, and you.

PINCH.   Well then, fare you well; and play with any man's honour but mine, kiss any man's wife but mine, and welcome.

[*exit* MR. PINCHWIFE]

HORN.   Ha! ha! ha! Doctor.

QUACK.   It seems he has not heard the report of you, or does not believe it.

HORN.   Ha! ha!—now, Doctor, what think you?

QUACK.   Pray let's see the letter—hum—[*reads the letter*]—"for—dear—love you——"

HORN.   I wonder how she could contrive it! What say'st thou to't? 'Tis an original.

QUACK.   So are your cuckolds, too, originals: for they are like no other common cuckolds, and I will henceforth believe it not impossible for you to cuckold the Grand Signior amidst his guards of eunuchs, that I say.

HORN.   And I say for the letter, 'tis the first love-letter that ever was without flames, darts, fates, destinies, lying and dissembling in't.

*Enter* SPARKISH *pulling in* MR. PINCHWIFE

SPARK.    Come back, you are a pretty brother-in-law, neither go to church nor to dinner with your sister bride!

PINCH.    My sister denies her marriage, and you see is gone away from you dissatisfied.

SPARK.    Pshaw! upon a foolish scruple, that our parson was not in lawful orders, and did not say all the common prayer; but 'tis her modesty only I believe. But let women be never so modest the first day, they'll be sure to come to themselves by night, and I shall have enough of her then. In the meantime, Harry Horner, you must dine with me: I keep my wedding at my aunt's in the Piazza.

HORN.    Thy wedding! what stale maid has lived to despair of a husband, or what young one of a gallant?

SPARK.    Oh, your servant, Sir—this gentleman's sister then,—no stale maid.

HORN.    I'm sorry for't.

PINCH. [*aside*]    How comes he so concerned for her?

SPARK.    You sorry for't? Why, do you know any ill by her?

HORN.    No, I know none but by thee; 'tis for her sake, not yours, and another man's sake that might have hoped, I thought.

SPARK.    Another man! another man! What is his name?

HORN.    Nay, since 'tis past, he shall be nameless.—[*aside*] Poor Harcourt! I am sorry thou hast missed her.

PINCH. [*aside*]    He seems to be much troubled at the match.

SPARK.    Prithee, tell me—— Nay, you shan't go, Brother.

PINCH.    I must of necessity, but I'll come to you to dinner.

[*exit* PINCHWIFE]

SPARK.    But, Harry, what, have I a rival in my wife already? But with all my heart, for he may be of use to me hereafter; for though my hunger is now my sauce, and I can fall on heartily without, the time will come when a rival will be as good sauce for a married man to a wife, as an orange to veal.

HORN.    O thou damned rogue! thou hast set my teeth on edge with thy orange.

SPARK.    Then let's to dinner—there I was with you again. Come.

HORN.    But who dines with thee?

SPARK.    My friends and relations, my brother Pinchwife, you see, of your acquaintance.

HORN.    And his wife?

SPARK.    No, 'gad, he'll ne'er let her come amongst us good fellows; your stingy country coxcomb keeps his wife from his friends, as he does his little firkin of ale for his own drinking, and a gentleman can't get a smack on't; but his servants, when his back is turned, broach it at their pleasures, and dust it away, ha! ha! ha!—'Gad, I am witty, I think, considering I was married to-day, by the world; but come——

HORN.    No, I will not dine with you, unless you can fetch her too.

SPARK.    Pshaw! what pleasure canst thou have with women now, Harry?

HORN.    My eyes are not gone; I love a good prospect yet, and will not dine with you unless she does too; go fetch her, therefore, but do not tell her husband 'tis for my sake.

SPARK.    Well, I'll go try what I can do; in the meantime, come away to my aunt's lodging, 'tis in the way to Pinchwife's.

HORN.    The poor woman has called for aid, and stretched forth her hand, Doctor; I cannot but help her over the pale out of the briars.

[*exeunt* SPARKISH, HORNER, QUACK]


## SCENE IV

*The Scene changes to* PINCHWIFE'S *House*

MRS. PINCHWIFE *alone, leaning on her elbow. A table, pen, ink, and paper*

MRS. PINCH.    Well, 'tis e'en so, I have got the London disease they call love; I am sick of my husband, and for my gallant. I have heard this distemper called a fever, but methinks 'tis like an ague; for when I think of my husband, I tremble, and am in a cold sweat, and have inclinations to vomit; but when I think of my gallant, dear Mr. Horner, my hot fit comes, and I am all in a fever indeed; and, as in other fevers, my own chamber is tedious to me, and I would fain be removed to his, and then methinks I should be well. Ah, poor Mr. Horner! Well, I cannot, will not stay here; therefore I'll make an end of my letter to him, which shall be a finer letter than my last, because I have studied it like anything. Oh sick, sick!                                                           [*takes the pen and writes*]

*Enter* PINCHWIFE, *who, seeing her writing, steals softly behind her, and, looking over her shoulder, snatches the paper from her*

PINCH.    What, writing more letters?

MRS. PINCH.    O Lord, bud, why d'ye fright me so?

[*she offers to run out; he stops her, and reads*]

PINCH.    How's this? nay, you shall not stir, Madam:—"Dear, dear, dear Mr. Horner"—very well—I have taught you to write letters to good purpose—but let's see't. "First, I am to beg your pardon for my boldness in writing to you, which I'd have you to know I would not have done, had not you said first you loved me so extremely, which if you do, you will never suffer me to lie in the arms of another man whom I loathe, nauseate, and detest."—Now you can write these filthy words. But what follows?—"Therefore, I hope you will speedily find some way to free me from this unfortunate match, which was never, I assure you, of my choice, but I'm afraid 'tis already too far gone; however, if you love me, as I do you, you will try what you can do; but you must help me away before to-morrow, or else, alas! I shall be for ever out of your reach, for I can defer no longer our—our——" [*the letter concludes*] what is to follow "our"?—speak, what?—Our journey into the country I suppose—Oh woman, damned woman! and Love, damned Love, their old tempter! for this is one of his miracles; in a moment he can make those blind that could see, and those see that were blind, those dumb that could speak, and those prattle who were dumb before; nay, what is more than all, make these dough-baked, senseless, indocile animals, women, too hard for us, their politic lords and rulers, in a moment. But make an end of your letter, and then I'll make an end of you thus, and all my plagues together.                                           [*draws his sword*]

MRS. PINCH.   O Lord, O Lord, you are such a passionate man, bud!

*Enter* SPARKISH

SPARK.   How now, what's here to do?

PINCH.   This fool here now!

SPARK.   What! drawn upon your wife? You should never do that, but at night in the dark, when you can't hurt her. This is my sister-in-law, is it not? ay, faith, e'en our country Margery [*pulls aside her handkerchief*]; one may know her. Come, she and you must go dine with me; dinner's ready, come. But where's my wife? Is she not come home yet? Where is she?

PINCH.   Making you a cuckold; 'tis that they all do, as soon as they can.

SPARK.   What, the wedding-day? No, a wife that designs to make a cully of her husband will be sure to let him win the first stake of love, by the world. But come, they stay dinner for us: come, I'll lead down our Margery.

MRS. PINCH.   No—Sir, go, we'll follow you.

SPARK.   I will not wag without you.

PINCH. [*aside*]   This coxcomb is a sensible torment to me amidst the greatest in the world.

SPARK.   Come, come, Madam Margery.

PINCH.   No; I'll lead her my way: what, would you treat your friends with mine, for want of your own wife?—[*leads her to t'other door, and locks her in and returns*] I am contented my rage should take breath——

SPARK. [*aside*]   I told Horner this.

PINCH.   Come now.

SPARK. Lord, how shy you are of your wife! But let me tell you, Brother, we men of wit have amongst us a saying that cuckolding, like the small-pox, comes with a fear; and you may keep your wife as much as you will out of danger of infection, but if her constitution incline her to't, she'll have it sooner or later, by the world, say they.

PINCH. [*aside*] What a thing is a cuckold, that every fool can make him ridiculous!——Well, Sir—but let me advise you, now you are come to be concerned, because you suspect the danger, not to neglect the means to prevent it, especially when the greatest share of the malady will light upon your own head, for

> Hows'e'er the kind wife's belly comes to swell,
> The husband breeds for her, and first is ill.

# ACT V

## SCENE I

### MR. PINCHWIFE'S *House*

*Enter* MR. PINCHWIFE *and* MRS. PINCHWIFE. *A table and candle*

PINCH.   Come, take the pen and make an end of the letter, just as you intended; if you are false in a tittle, I shall soon perceive it, and punish you with this as you deserve.—[*lays his hand on his sword*] Write what was to follow—let's see—"You must make haste, and help me away before to-morrow, or else I shall be for ever out of your reach, for I can defer no longer our"—What follows "our"?

MRS. PINCH.   Must all out, then, bud?—Look you there, then.

[MRS. PINCHWIFE *takes the pen and writes*]

PINCH.   Let's see—"For I can defer no longer our—wedding—Your slighted Alithea."—What's the meaning of this? my sister's name to't? Speak, unriddle.

MRS. PINCH.   Yes, indeed, bud.

PINCH.   But why her name to't? Speak—speak, I say.

MRS. PINCH.   Ay, but you'll tell her then again. If you would not tell her again——

PINCH.   I will not:—I am stunned, my head turns round.—Speak.

MRS. PINCH.   Won't you tell her, indeed, and indeed?

PINCH.   No; speak, I say.

MRS. PINCH.   She'll be angry with me; but I had rather she should be angry with me than you, bud; and, to tell you the truth, 'twas she made me write the letter, and taught me what I should write.

PINCH. [*aside*]   Ha! I thought the style was somewhat better than her own.—— But how could she come to you to teach you, since I had locked you up alone?

MRS. PINCH.   Oh, through the keyhole, bud.

PINCH.   But why should she make you write a letter for her to him, since she can write herself?

MRS. PINCH.   Why, she said because—for I was unwilling to do it——

67

PINCH. Because what—because?

MRS. PINCH. Because, lest Mr. Horner should be cruel, and refuse her; or be vain afterwards, and show the letter, she might disown it, the hand not being hers.

PINCH. [*aside*] How's this? Ha!—then I think I shall come to myself again. This changeling could not invent this lie: but if she could, why should she? she might think I should soon discover it.—Stay—now I think on't too, Horner said he was sorry she had married Sparkish; and her disowning her marriage to me makes me think she has evaded it for Horner's sake: yet why should she take this course? But men in love are fools; women may well be so—— But hark you, Madam, your sister went out in the morning, and I have not seen her within since.

MRS. PINCH. Alack-a-day, she has been crying all day above, it seems, in a corner.

PINCH. Where is she? Let me speak with her.

MRS. PINCH. [*aside*] O Lord, then she'll discover all!—— Pray hold, bud; what, d'ye mean to discover me? she'll know I have told you then. Pray, bud, let me talk with her first.

PINCH. I must speak with her, to know whether Horner ever made her any promise, and whether she be married to Sparkish or no.

MRS. PINCH. Pray, dear bud, don't, till I have spoken with her, and told her that I have told you all; for she'll kill me else.

PINCH. Go then, and bid her come out to me.

MRS. PINCH. Yes, yes, bud.

PINCH. Let me see——

MRS. PINCH. [*aside*] I'll go, but she is not within to come to him: I have just got time to know of Lucy her maid, who first set me on work, what lie I shall tell next; for I am e'en at my wit's end.

[*exit* MRS. PINCHWIFE]

PINCH. Well, I resolve it, Horner shall have her: I'd rather give him my sister than lend him my wife; and such an alliance will prevent his pretensions to my wife, sure. I'll make him of kin to her, and then he won't care for her.

MRS. PINCHWIFE *returns*

MRS. PINCH. O Lord, bud! I told you what anger you would make me with my sister.

PINCH. Won't she come hither?

MRS. PINCH. No, no. Alack-a-day, she's ashamed to look you in the face: and she says, if you go in to her, she'll run away downstairs, and shamefully go herself to Mr. Horner, who has promised her marriage, she says; and she will have no other, so she won't.

PINCH. Did he so?—promise her marriage!—then she shall have no other. Go tell her so; and if she will come and discourse with me a little concerning the means, I will about it immediately. Go.—[*exit* MRS. PINCHWIFE] His estate is equal to Sparkish's, and his extraction as much better than his as his parts are; but my chief reason is I'd rather be akin to him by the name of brother-in-law than that of cuckold.

*Enter* MRS. PINCHWIFE

Well, what says she now?

MRS. PINCH.    Why, she says, she would only have you lead her to Horner's lodging; with whom she first will discourse the matter before she talks with you, which yet she cannot do; for alack, poor creature, she says she can't so much as look you in the face, therefore she'll come to you in a mask. And you must excuse her if she make you no answer to any question of yours, till you have brought her to Mr. Horner; and if you will not chide her, nor question her, she'll come out to you immediately.

PINCH.    Let her come: I will not speak a word to her, nor require a word from her.

MRS. PINCH.    Oh, I forgot: besides, she says she cannot look you in the face, though through a mask; therefore would desire you to put out the candle.

PINCH.    I agree to all. Let her make haste.—There, 'tis out.—[*puts out the candle; exit* MRS. PINCHWIFE] My case is something better: I'd rather fight with Horner for not lying with my sister, than for lying with my wife; and of the two, I had rather find my sister too forward than my wife. I expected no other from her free education, as she calls it, and her passion for the town. Well, wife and sister are names which make us expect love and duty, pleasure and comfort; but we find 'em plagues and torments, and are equally, though differently, troublesome to their keeper; for we have as much ado to get people to lie with our sisters as to keep 'em from lying with our wives.

*Enter* MRS. PINCHWIFE *masked, and in hoods and scarfs, and a night-gown and petticoat of* ALITHEA's, *in the dark*

What, are you come, Sister? let us go then.—But first, let me lock up my wife. Mrs. Margery, where are you?

MRS. PINCH.    Here, bud.

PINCH.    Come hither, that I may lock you up: get you in.—[*locks the door*] Come, Sister, where are you now?

[MRS. PINCHWIFE *gives him her hand; but when he lets her go,
she steals softly on to t'other side of him,
and is led away by him for his sister,* ALITHEA]

## SCENE II

*The Scene changes to* HORNER'S *Lodging*

QUACK, HORNER

QUACK. What, all alone? not so much as one of your cuckolds here, nor one of their wives! They use to take their turns with you, as if they were to watch you.

HORN. Yes, it often happens that a cuckold is but his wife's spy, and is more upon family duty when he is with her gallant abroad, hindering his pleasure, than when he is at home with her playing the gallant. But the hardest duty a married woman imposes upon a lover is keeping her husband company always.

QUACK. And his fondness wearies you almost as soon as hers.

HORN. A pox! keeping a cuckold company, after you have had his wife, is as tiresome as the company of a country squire to a witty fellow of the town, when he has got all his money.

QUACK. And as at first a man makes a friend of the husband to get the wife, so at last you are fain to fall out with the wife to be rid of the husband.

HORN. Ay, most cuckold-makers are true courtiers; when once a poor man has cracked his credit for 'em, they can't abide to come near him.

QUACK. But at first, to draw him in, are so sweet, so kind, so dear! just as you are to Pinchwife. But what becomes of that intrigue with his wife?

HORN. A pox! he's as surly as an alderman that has been bit; and since he's so coy, his wife's kindness is in vain, for she's a silly innocent.

QUACK. Did she not send you a letter by him?

HORN. Yes; but that's a riddle I have not yet solved. Allow the poor creature to be willing, she is silly too, and he keeps her up so close——

QUACK. Yes, so close, that he makes her but the more willing, and adds but revenge to her love; which two, when met, seldom fail of satisfying each other one way or other.

HORN. What! here's the man we are talking of, I think.

*Enter* MR. PINCHWIFE, *leading in his Wife masked, muffled, and in her Sister's gown*

Pshaw!

QUACK. Bringing his wife to you is the next thing to bringing a love letter from her.

HORN. What means this?

PINCH. The last time, you know, Sir, I brought you a love letter; now, you see, a mistress; I think you'll say I am a civil man to you.

HORN.    Ay, the devil take me, will I say thou art the civilest man I ever met with; and I have known some. I fancy I understand thee now better than I did the letter. But, hark thee, in thy ear——

PINCH.    What?

HORN.    Nothing but the usual question, man: is she sound, on thy word?

PINCH.    What, you take her for a wench, and me for a pimp?

HORN.    Pshaw! wench and pimp, paw words; I know thou art an honest fellow, and hast a great acquaintance among the ladies, and perhaps hast made love for me, rather than let me make love to thy wife.

PINCH.    Come, Sir, in short, I am for no fooling.

HORN.    Nor I neither: therefore prithee, let's see her face presently. Make her show, man: art thou sure I don't know her?

PINCH.    I am sure you do know her.

HORN.    A pox! why dost thou bring her to me then?

PINCH.    Because she's a relation of mine——

HORN.    Is she, faith, man? then thou art still more civil and obliging, dear rogue.

PINCH.    Who desired me to bring her to you.

HORN.    Then she is obliging, dear rogue.

PINCH.    You'll make her welcome for my sake, I hope.

HORN.    I hope she is handsome enough to make herself welcome. Prithee let her unmask.

PINCH.    Do you speak to her; she would never be ruled by me.

HORN.    Madam—— [MRS. PINCHWIFE whispers to HORNER] She says she must speak with me in private. Withdraw, prithee.

PINCH. [aside]    She's unwilling, it seems, I should know all her undecent conduct in this business.—— Well then, I'll leave you together, and hope when I am gone, you'll agree; if not, you and I shan't agree, Sir.

HORN.    What means the fool? if she and I agree 'tis no matter what you and I do.          [whispers to MRS. PINCHWIFE,
                         who makes signs with her hand for him to be gone]

PINCH.    In the meantime I'll fetch a parson, and find out Sparkish, and disabuse him. You would have me fetch a parson, would you not? Well then—now I think I am rid of her, and shall have no more trouble with her—our sisters and daughters, like usurers' money, are safest when put out; but our wives, like their writings, never safe but in our closets under lock and key.          [exit MR. PINCHWIFE]

*Enter Boy*

BOY.    Sir Jasper Fidget, Sir, is coming up.          [exit]

HORN.    Here's the trouble of a cuckold now we are talking of. A pox on him! has he not enough to do to hinder his wife's sport, but he must other women's too?——Step in here, Madam.     [*exit* MRS. PINCHWIFE]

*Enter* SIR JASPER

SIR JASP.     My best and dearest friend.

HORN. [*aside to* QUACK]     The old style, Doctor.—— Well, be short, for I am busy. What would your impertinent wife have now?

SIR JASP.     Well guessed, i'faith; for I do come from her.

HORN.     To invite me to supper! Tell her, I can't come: go.

SIR JASP.     Nay, now you are out, faith; for my lady, and the whole knot of the virtuous gang, as they call themselves, are resolved upon a frolic of coming to you to-night in masquerade, and are all dressed already.

HORN.     I shan't be at home.

SIR JASP. [*aside*]     Lord, how churlish he is to women!—— Nay, prithee don't disappoint 'em; they'll think 'tis my fault: prithee don't. I'll send in the banquet and the fiddles. But make no noise on't; for the poor virtuous rogues would not have it known, for the world, that they go a-masquerading; and they would come to no man's ball but yours.

HORN.     Well, well—get you gone; and tell 'em, if they come, 'twill be at the peril of their honour and yours.

SIR JASP.     He! he! he!—we'll trust you for that: farewell.

[*exit* SIR JASPER]

HORN.     Doctor, anon you too shall be my guest,
         But now I'm going to a private feast.     [*exeunt*]

## SCENE III

*The Scene changes to the Piazza of Covent Garden*

SPARKISH, PINCHWIFE

SPARK. [*with the letter in his hand*]     But who would have thought a woman could have been false to me? By the world, I could not have thought it.

PINCH.     You were for giving and taking liberty: she has taken it only, Sir, now you find in that letter. You are a frank person, and so is she, you see there.

SPARK.     Nay, if this be her hand—for I never saw it.

PINCH.     'Tis no matter whether that be her hand or no; I am sure this hand, at her desire, led her to Mr. Horner, with whom I left her just now, to go fetch a parson to 'em at their desire too, to deprive you of her for ever; for it seems yours was but a mock marriage.

SPARK.     Indeed, she would needs have it that 'twas Harcourt himself, in a parson's habit, that married us; but I'm sure he told me 'twas his brother Ned.

PINCH.   Oh, there 'tis out; and you were deceived, not she: for you are such a frank person. But I must be gone.—You'll find her at Mr. Horner's. Go, and believe your eyes.                    [*exit* MR. PINCHWIFE]

SPARK.   Nay, I'll to her, and call her as many crocodiles, sirens, harpies, and other heathenish names, as a poet would do a mistress who had refused to hear his suit, nay more, his verses on her.—But stay, is not that she following a torch at t'other end of the Piazza? and from Horner's certainly—'tis so.

*Enter* ALITHEA *following a torch, and* LUCY *behind*

You are well met, Madam, though you don't think so. What, you have made a short visit to Mr. Horner? But I suppose you'll return to him presently; by that time the parson can be with him.

ALITH.   Mr. Horner and the parson, Sir!

SPARK.   Come, Madam, no more dissembling, no more jilting; for I am no more a frank person.

ALITH.   How's this?

LUCY. [*aside*]   So, 'twill work, I see.

SPARK.   Could you find out no easy country fool to abuse? none but me, a gentleman of wit and pleasure about the town? But it was your pride to be too hard for a man of parts, unworthy false woman! false as a friend that lends a man money to lose; false as dice, who undo those that trust all they have to 'em.

LUCY [*aside*]   He has been a great bubble, by his similes, as they say.

ALITH.   You have been too merry, Sir, at your wedding-dinner, sure.

SPARK.   What, d'ye mock me too?

ALITH.   Or you have been deluded.

SPARK.   By you.

ALITH.   Let me understand you.

SPARK.   Have you the confidence—I should call it something else, since you know your guilt—to stand my just reproaches? You did not write an impudent letter to Mr. Horner? who I find now has clubbed with you in deluding me with his aversion for women, that I might not, forsooth, suspect him for my rival.

LUCY. [*aside*]   D'ye think the gentleman can be jealous now, Madam?

ALITH.   I write a letter to Mr. Horner!

SPARK.   Nay, Madam, do not deny it. Your brother showed it me just now; and told me likewise, he left you at Horner's lodging to fetch a parson to marry you to him: and I wish you joy, Madam, joy, joy; and to him too, much joy; and to myself more joy, for not marrying you.

ALITH. [*aside*]   So, I find my brother would break off the match; and I can consent to't, since I see this gentleman can be made jealous.—— O Lucy, by his rude usage and jealousy, he makes me almost afraid I am married to him. Art thou sure 'twas Harcourt himself, and no parson, that married us?

SPARK.   No, Madam, I thank you. I suppose, that was a contrivance too of Mr. Horner's and yours, to make Harcourt play the parson; but I would as little as you have him one now, no, not for the world. For shall I tell you another truth? I never had any passion for you till now, for now I hate you. 'Tis true, I might have married your portion, as other men of parts of the town do sometimes: and so, your servant. And to show my unconcernedness, I'll come to your wedding, and resign you with as much joy as I would a stale wench to a new cully; nay, with as much joy as I would after the first night, if I had been married to you. There's for you; and so your servant, servant. [*exit* SPARKISH]

ALITH.   How was I deceived in a man!

LUCY.   You'll believe then a fool may be made jealous now? for that easiness in him that suffers him to be led by a wife, will likewise permit him to be persuaded against her by others.

ALITH.   But marry Mr. Horner! my brother does not intend it, sure: if I thought he did, I would take thy advice, and Mr. Harcourt for my husband. And now I wish that if there be any over-wise woman of the town, who, like me, would marry a fool for fortune, liberty, or title, first, that her husband may love play, and be a cully to all the town but her, and suffer none but Fortune to be mistress of his purse; then, if for liberty, that he may send her into the country, under the conduct of some huswifely mother-in-law; and if for title, may the world give 'em none but that of cuckold.

LUCY.   And for her greater curse, Madam, may he not deserve it.

ALITH.   Away, impertinent! Is not this my old Lady Lanterlu's?

LUCY.   Yes, Madam.—[*aside*] And here I hope we shall find Mr. Harcourt. [*exeunt*]

## SCENE IV

*The Scene changes again to* HORNER'S *Lodging*

HORNER, LADY FIDGET, MRS. DAINTY FIDGET, MRS. SQUEAMISH

*A table, banquet, and bottles*

HORN. [*aside*]   A pox! they are come too soon—before I have sent back my new mistress. All I have now to do is to lock her in, that they may not see her.

LADY FID.   That we may be sure of our welcome, we have brought our entertainment with us, and are resolved to treat thee, dear toad.

MRS. DAIN.   And that we may be merry to purpose, have left Sir Jasper and my old Lady Squeamish quarrelling at home at backgammon.

MRS. SQUEAM.   Therefore let us make use of our time, lest they should chance to interrupt us.

LADY FID.   Let us sit then.

HORN.   First, that you may be private, let me lock this door and that, and I'll wait upon you presently.

LADY FID.   No, Sir, shut 'em only, and your lips for ever; for we must trust you as much as our women.

HORN.   You know all vanity's killed in me; I have no occasion for talking.

LADY FID.   Now, ladies, supposing we had drank each of us two bottles, let us speak the truth of our hearts.

MRS. DAIN. and MRS. SQUEAM.   Agreed.

LADY FID.   By this brimmer, for truth is nowhere else to be found— [*aside to* HORNER] not in thy heart, false man!

HORN. [*aside to* Lady Fidget]   You have found me a true man, I'm sure.

LADY FID. [*aside to* HORNER]   Not every way.—— But let us sit and be merry.                                    [LADY FIDGET *sings*]

1

Why should our damn'd tyrants oblige us to live
On the pittance of pleasure which they only give?
    We must not rejoice
    With wine and with noise:
In vain we must wake in a dull bed alone,
Whilst to our warm rival the bottle, they're gone.
    Then lay aside charms,
    And take up these arms.★

2

'Tis wine only gives 'em their courage and wit;
Because we live sober, to men we submit.
    If for beauties you'd pass,
    Take a lick of the glass,
'Twill mend your complexions, and when they are gone,
  The best red we have is the red of the grape:
Then, sisters, lay't on,
    And damn a good shape.

---

★The glasses.

MRS. DAIN. Dear brimmer! Well, in token of our openness and plain-dealing, let us throw our masks over our heads.

HORN. So, 'twill come to the glasses anon.

MRS. SQUEAM. Lovely brimmer! let me enjoy him first.

LADY FID. No, I never part with a gallant till I've tried him. Dear brimmer! that makest our husbands short-sighted.

MRS. DAIN. And our bashful gallants bold.

MRS. SQUEAM. And, for want of a gallant, the butler lovely in our eyes.—— Drink, eunuch.

LADY FID. Drink, thou representative of a husband.—Damn a husband!

MRS. DAIN. And, as it were a husband, an old keeper.

MRS. SQUEAM. And an old grandmother.

HORN. And an English bawd, and a French chirurgeon.

LADY FID. Ay, we have all reason to curse 'em.

HORN. For my sake, ladies?

LADY FID. No, for our own; for the first spoils all young gallants' industry.

MRS. DAIN. And the other's art makes 'em bold only with common women.

MRS. SQUEAM. And rather run the hazard of the vile distemper amongst them, than of a denial amongst us.

MRS. DAIN. The filthy toads choose mistresses now as they do stuffs, for having been fancied and worn by others.

MRS. SQUEAM. For being common and cheap.

LADY FID. Whilst women of quality, like the richest stuffs, lie untumbled, and unasked for.

HORN. Ay, neat, and cheap, and new, often they think best.

MRS. DAIN. No, Sir, the beasts will be known by a mistress longer than by a suit.

MRS. SQUEAM. And 'tis not for cheapness neither.

LADY FID. No; for the vain fops will take up druggets and embroider 'em. But I wonder at the depraved appetites of witty men; they use to be out of the common road, and hate imitation. Pray tell me, beast, when you were a man, why you rather chose to club with a multitude in a common house for an entertainment than to be the only guest at a good table.

HORN. Why, faith, ceremony and expectation are unsufferable to those that are sharp bent. People always eat with the best stomach at an ordinary, where every man is snatching for the best bit.

LADY FID. Though he get a cut over the fingers.—But I have heard people eat most heartily of another man's meat, that is, what they do not pay for.

HORN.    When they are sure of their welcome and freedom; for ceremony in love and eating is as ridiculous as in fighting: falling on briskly is all should be done on those occasions.

LADY FID.    Well then, let me tell you, Sir, there is nowhere more freedom than in our houses; and we take freedom from a young person as a sign of good breeding; and a person may be as free as he pleases with us, as frolic, as gamesome, as wild as he will.

HORN.    Han't I heard you all declaim against wild men?

LADY FID.    Yes; but for all that, we think wildness in a man as desirable a quality as in a duck or rabbit: a tame man! foh!

HORN.    I know not, but your reputations frightened me as much as your faces invited me.

LADY FID.    Our reputation! Lord, why should you not think that we women make use of our reputation, as you men of yours, only to deceive the world with less suspicion? Our virtue is like the statesman's religion, the Quaker's word, the gamester's oath, and the great man's honour—but to cheat those that trust us.

MRS. SQUEAM.    And that demureness, coyness, and modesty that you see in our faces in the boxes at plays, is as much a sign of a kind woman, as a vizard-mask in the pit.

MRS. DAIN.    For, I assure you, women are least masked when they have the velvet vizard on.

LADY FID.    You would have found us modest women in our denials only.

MRS. SQUEAM.    Our bashfulness is only the reflection of the men's.

MRS. DAIN. ·  We blush when they are shamefaced.

HORN.    I beg your pardon, ladies, I was deceived in you devilishly. But why that mighty pretence to honour?

LADY FID.    We have told you; but sometimes 'twas for the same reason you men pretend business often, to avoid ill company, to enjoy the better and more privately those you love.

HORN.    But why would you ne'er give a friend a wink then?

LADY FID.    Faith, your reputation frightened us as much as ours did you, you were so notoriously lewd.

HORN.    And you so seemingly honest.

LADY FID.    Was that all that deterred you?

HORN.    And so expensive—you allow freedom, you say——

LADY FID.    Ay, ay.

HORN.    That I was afraid of losing my little money, as well as my little time, both which my other pleasures required.

LADY FID.    Money! foh! you talk like a little fellow now: do such as we expect money?

HORN.    I beg your pardon, Madam, I must confess, I have heard that great ladies, like great merchants, set but the higher prices upon what they have, because they are not in necessity of taking the first offer.

MRS. DAIN.   Such as we make sale of our hearts?

MRS. SQUEAM.   We bribed for our love? foh!

HORN.   With your pardon, ladies, I know, like great men in offices, you seem to exact flattery and attendance only from your followers; but you have receivers about you, and such fees to pay, a man is afraid to pass your grants. Besides, we must let you win at cards, or we lose your hearts; and if you make an assignation, 'tis at a goldsmith's, jeweller's, or china-house; where for your honour you deposit to him, he must pawn his to the punctual cit, and so paying for what you take up, pays for what he takes up.

MRS. DAIN.   Would you not have us assured of our gallants' love?

MRS. SQUEAM.   For love is better known by liberality than by jealousy.

LADY FID.   For one may be dissembled, the other not.—[*aside*] But my jealousy can be no longer dissembled, and they are telling ripe.—— Come, here's to our gallants in waiting, whom we must name, and I'll begin. This is my false rogue.                          [*claps him on the back*]

MRS. SQUEAM.   How!

HORN.   So, all will out now.

MRS. SQUEAM. [*aside to* HORNER]   Did you not tell me 'twas for my sake only you reported yourself no man?

MRS. DAIN. [*aside to* HORNER]   Oh, wretch! did you not swear to me, 'twas for my love and honour you passed for that thing you do?

HORN.   So, so.

LADY FID.   Come, speak, ladies: this is my false villain.

MRS. SQUEAM.   And mine too.

MRS. DAIN.   And mine.

HORN.   Well then, you are all three my false rogues too, and there's an end on't.

LADY FID.   Well then, there's no remedy; sister sharers, let us not fall out, but have a care of our honour. Though we get no presents, no jewels of him, we are savers of our honour, the jewel of most value and use, which shines yet to the world unsuspected, though it be counterfeit.

HORN.   Nay, and is e'en as good as if it were true, provided the world think so; for honour, like beauty now, only depends on the opinion of others.

LADY FID.   Well, Harry Common, I hope you can be true to three. Swear; but 'tis to no purpose to require your oath, for you are as often forsworn as you swear to new women.

HORN.   Come, faith, Madam, let us e'en pardon one another; for all the difference I find betwixt we men and you women, we forswear ourselves at the beginning of an amour, you as long as it lasts.

*Enter* SIR JASPER FIDGET, *and* OLD LADY SQUEAMISH

SIR JASP.   Oh, my Lady Fidget, was this your cunning, to come to Mr. Horner without me? But you have been nowhere else, I hope.

LADY FID.   No, Sir Jasper.

LADY SQUEAM.   And you came straight hither, Biddy?

MRS. SQUEAM.   Yes, indeed, lady Grandmother.

SIR JASP.   'Tis well, 'tis well; I knew when once they were thoroughly acquainted with poor Horner, they'd ne'er be from him: you may let her masquerade it with my wife and Horner, and I warrant her reputation safe.

*Enter Boy*

BOY.   O Sir, here's the gentleman come, whom you bid me not suffer to come up without giving you notice, with a lady too, and other gentlemen.

HORN.   Do you all go in there, whilst I send 'em away; and, boy, do you desire 'em to stay below till I come, which shall be immediately.

[*exeunt* SIR JASPER, LADY SQUEAMISH, LADY FIDGET, MRS. DAINTY, MRS. SQUEAMISH]

BOY.   Yes, sir.                                                            [*exit*]

[*exit* HORNER *at t'other door, and returns with* MRS. PINCHWIFE]

HORN.   You would not take my advice, to be gone home before your husband came back; he'll now discover all. Yet pray, my dearest, be persuaded to go home, and leave the rest to my management; I'll let you down the back way.

MRS. PINCH.   I don't know the way home, so I don't.

HORN.   My man shall wait upon you.

MRS. PINCH.   No, don't you believe that I'll go at all; what, are you weary of me already?

HORN.   No, my life, 'tis that I may love you long, 'tis to secure my love, and your reputation with your husband; he'll never receive you again else.

MRS. PINCH.   What care I? d'ye think to frighten me with that? I don't intend to go to him again; you shall be my husband now.

HORN.   I cannot be your husband, dearest, since you are married to him.

MRS. PINCH.   Oh, would you make me believe that? Don't I see every day at London here, women leave their first husbands, and go and live with other men as their wives? Pish, pshaw! you'd make me angry, but that I love you so mainly.

HORN.   So, they are coming up—In again, in, I hear 'em.—[*exit*

MRS. PINCHWIFE] Well, a silly mistress is like a weak place, soon got, soon lost, a man has scarce time for plunder; she betrays her husband first to her gallant, and then her gallant to her husband.

*Enter* PINCHWIFE, ALITHEA, HARCOURT, SPARKISH, LUCY, *and a* PARSON

PINCH. Come, Madam, 'tis not the sudden change of your dress, the confidence of your asseverations, and your false witness there, shall persuade me I did not bring you hither just now; here's my witness, who cannot deny it, since you must be confronted.—— Mr. Horner, did not I bring this lady to you just now?

HORN. [*aside*] Now must I wrong one woman for another's sake— but that's no new thing with me, for in these cases I am still on the criminal's side against the innocent.

ALITH. Pray speak, Sir.

HORN. [*aside*] It must be so. I must be impudent, and try my luck; impudence uses to be too hard for truth.

PINCH. What, you are studying an evasion or excuse for her! Speak, Sir.

HORN. No, faith, I am something backward only to speak in women's affairs or disputes.

PINCH. She bids you speak.

ALITH. Ah, pray, Sir, do, pray satisfy him.

HORN. Then truly, you did bring that lady to me just now.

PINCH. Oh ho!

ALITH. How, Sir?

HAR. How, Horner?

ALITH. What mean you, Sir? I always took you for a man of honour.

HORN. [*aside*] Ay, so much a man of honour, that I must save my mistress, I thank you, come what will on't.

SPARK. So, if I had had her, she'd have made me believe the moon had been made of a Christmas pie.

LUCY. [*aside*] Now could I speak, if I durst, and solve the riddle, who am the author of it.

ALITH. Oh unfortunate woman! A combination against my honour! which most concerns me now, because you share in my disgrace, Sir, and it is your censure, which I must now suffer, that troubles me, not theirs.

HAR. Madam, then have no trouble, you shall now see 'tis possible for me to love too, without being jealous; I will not only believe your innocence myself, but make all the world believe it.—[*apart to* HORNER] Horner, I must now be concerned for this lady's honour.

HORN. And I must be concerned for a lady's honour too.

HAR. This lady has her honour, and I will protect it.

HORN. My lady has not her honour, but has given it me to keep, and I will preserve it.

HAR.  I understand you not.

HORN.  I would not have you.

MRS. PINCH. [*peeping in behind*]  What's the matter with 'em all?

PINCH.  Come, come, Mr. Horner, no more disputing; here's the parson, I brought him not in vain.

HAR.  No, Sir, I'll employ him, if this lady please.

PINCH.  How! what d'ye mean?

SPARK.  Ay, what does he mean?

HORN.  Why, I have resigned your sister to him; he has my consent.

PINCH.  But he has not mine, Sir; a woman's injured honour, no more than a man's, can be repaired or satisfied by any but him that first wronged it; and you shall marry her presently, or——

                                        [*lays his hand on his sword*]

### Enter to them MRS. PINCHWIFE

MRS. PINCH. [*aside*]  O Lord, they'll kill poor Mr. Horner! besides, he shan't marry her whilst I stand by, and look on; I'll not lose my second husband so.

PINCH.  What do I see?

ALITH.  My sister in my clothes!

SPARK.  Ha!

MRS. PINCH. [*to* MR. PINCHWIFE]  Nay, pray now don't quarrel about finding work for the parson: he shall marry me to Mr. Horner; for now, I believe, you have enough of me.

HORN. [*aside*]  Damned, damned loving changeling!

MRS. PINCH.  Pray, Sister, pardon me for telling so many lies of you.

HORN.  I suppose the riddle is plain now.

LUCY.  No, that must be my work.—— Good Sir, hear me.

[*kneels to* MR. PINCHWIFE, *who stands doggedly with his hat over his eyes*]

PINCH.  I will never hear woman again, but make 'em all silent thus——                                  [*offers to draw upon his Wife*]

HORN.  No, that must not be.

PINCH.  You then shall go first, 'tis all one to me.

                  [*offers to draw on* HORNER, *stopped by* HARCOURT]

HAR.  Hold!

### Enter SIR JASPER FIDGET, LADY FIDGET, LADY SQUEAMISH, MRS. DAINTY FIDGET, MRS. SQUEAMISH

SIR JASP.  What's the matter? what's the matter? pray, what's the matter, Sir? I beseech you communicate, Sir.

PINCH.  Why, my wife has communicated, Sir, as your wife may have done too, Sir, if she knows him, Sir.

SIR JASP.  Pshaw, with him! ha! ha! he!

PINCH.    D'ye mock me, Sir? A cuckold is a kind of a wild beast; have a care, Sir.

SIR JASP.    No, sure, you mock me, Sir. He cuckold you! it can't be, ha! ha! he! why, I'll tell you, Sir——            [*offers to whisper*]

PINCH.    I tell you again, he has whored my wife, and yours too, if he knows her, and all the women he comes near; 'tis not his dissembling, his hypocrisy, can wheedle me.

SIR JASP.    How! does he dissemble? is he a hypocrite? Nay, then—how—wife—sister, is he a hypocrite?

LADY SQUEAM.    An hypocrite! a dissembler! Speak, young harlotry, speak, how?

SIR JASP.    Nay, then—Oh my head too!—Oh thou libidinous lady!

LADY SQUEAM.    Oh thou harloting harlotry! hast thou done't then?

SIR JASP.    Speak, good Horner, art thou a dissembler, a rogue? hast thou——

HORN.    Soh!

LUCY. [*apart to* HORNER]    I'll fetch you off, and her too, if she will but hold her tongue.

HORN. [*apart to* LUCY]    Can'st thou? I'll give thee——

LUCY [*to* Mr. PINCHWIFE]    Pray have but patience to hear me, Sir, who am the unfortunate cause of all this confusion. Your wife is innocent, I only culpable; for I put her upon telling you all these lies concerning my mistress, in order to the breaking off the match between Mr. Sparkish and her, to make way for Mr. Harcourt.

SPARK.    Did you so, eternal rotten tooth? Then, it seems, my mistress was not false to me, I was only deceived by you. Brother, that should have been, now man of conduct, who is a frank person now, to bring your wife to her lover, ha?

LUCY.    I assure you, Sir, she came not to Mr. Horner out of love, for she loves him no more——

MRS. PINCH.    Hold, I told lies for you, but you shall tell none for me, for I do love Mr. Horner with all my soul, and nobody shall say me nay; pray, don't you go to make poor Mr. Horner believe to the contrary; 'tis spitefully done of you, I'm sure.

HORN. [*aside to* MRS. PINCHWIFE]    Peace, dear idiot.

MRS. PINCH.    Nay, I will not peace.

PINCH.    Not till I make you.

*Enter* DORILANT, QUACK

DOR.    Horner, your servant; I am the doctor's guest, he must excuse our intrusion.

QUACK.    But what's the matter, gentlemen? for Heaven's sake, what's the matter?

HORN. Oh, 'tis well you are come. 'Tis a censorious world we live in; you may have brought me a reprieve, or else I had died for a crime I never committed, and these innocent ladies had suffered with me; therefore, pray satisfy these worthy, honourable, jealous gentlemen—that——
                                                                    [whispers]

QUACK. Oh, I understand you, is that all?—— Sir Jasper, by Heavens, and upon the word of a physician, Sir—— [whispers to SIR JASPER]

SIR JASP. Nay, I do believe you truly.—— Pardon me, my virtuous lady, and dear of honour.

LADY SQUEAM. What, then all's right again?

SIR JASP. Ay, ay, and now let us satisfy him too.
                                          [they whisper with MR. PINCHWIFE]

PINCH. An eunuch! Pray, no fooling with me.

QUACK. I'll bring half the chirurgeons in town to swear it.

PINCH. They!—they'll swear a man that bled to death through his wounds died of an apoplexy.

QUACK. Pray, hear me, Sir—why, all the town has heard the report of him.

PINCH. But does all the town believe it?

QUACK. Pray, inquire a little, and first of all these.

PINCH. I'm sure when I left the town, he was the lewdest fellow in't.

QUACK. I tell you, Sir, he has been in France since; pray, ask but these ladies and gentlemen, your friend Mr. Dorilant. Gentlemen and ladies, han't you all heard the late sad report of poor Mr. Horner?

ALL THE LADIES. Ay, ay, ay.

DOR. Why, thou jealous fool, dost thou doubt it? he's an arrant French capon.

MRS. PINCH. 'Tis false, Sir, you shall not disparage poor Mr. Horner, for to my certain knowledge——

LUCY. Oh, hold!

MRS. SQUEAM. [aside to LUCY] Stop her mouth!

LADY FID. [to PINCHWIFE] Upon my honour, Sir, 'tis as true——

MRS. DAIN. D'ye think we would have been seen in his company?

MRS. SQUEAM. Trust our unspotted reputations with him?

LADY FID. [aside to HORNER] This you get, and we too, by trusting your secret to a fool.

HORN. Peace, Madam.—[aside to QUACK] Well, Doctor, is not this a good design, that carries man on unsuspected, and brings him off safe?

PINCH. [aside] Well, if this were true—but my wife——
                                          [DORILANT whispers with MRS. PINCHWIFE]

ALITH. Come, Brother, your wife is yet innocent, you see; but have a care of too strong an imagination, lest, like an over-concerned timorous gamester, by fancying an unlucky cast, it should come. Women and fortune are truest still to those that trust 'em.

LUCY.    And any wild thing grows but the more fierce and hungry for being kept up, and more dangerous to the keeper.

ALITH.    There's doctrine for all husbands, Mr. Harcourt.

HAR.    I edify, Madam, so much, that I am impatient till I am one.

DOR.    And I edify so much by example, I will never be one.

SPARK.    And because I will not disparage my parts, I'll ne'er be one.

HORN.    And I, alas! can't be one.

PINCH.    But I must be one—against my will to a country wife, with a country murrain to me!

MRS. PINCH. [*aside*]    And I must be a country wife still too, I find; for I can't, like a city one, be rid of my musty husband, and do what I list.

HORN.    Now, Sir, I must pronounce your wife innocent, though I blush whilst I do it; and I am the only man by her now exposed to shame, which I will straight drown in wine, as you shall your suspicion; and the ladies' troubles we'll divert with a ballad.—— Doctor, where are your maskers?

LUCY.    Indeed, she's innocent, Sir, I am her witness; and her end of coming out was but to see her sister's wedding; and what she has said to your face of her love to Mr. Horner was but the usual innocent revenge on a husband's jealousy—was it not, Madam, speak?

MRS. PINCH. [*aside to* LUCY *and* HORNER]    Since you'll have me tell more lies—— Yes, indeed, bud.

PINCH.

> For my own sake fain I would all believe;
> Cuckolds, like lovers, should themselves deceive.
> But—— [*sighs*] his honour is least safe (too late I find)
> Who trusts it with a foolish wife or friend.

*A Dance of Cuckolds*

HORN.

> Vain fops but court and dress, and keep a pother,
> To pass for women's men with one another;
> But he who aims by women to be priz'd,
> First by the men, you see, must be despis'd.

# EPILOGUE

*Spoken by* MY LADY FIDGET

Now you the vigorous, who daily here
O'er vizard-mask in public domineer,
And what you'd do to her, if in place where;
Nay, have the confidence to cry, "Come out!"
Yet when she says, "Lead on!" you are not stout;
But to your well-dress'd brother straight turn round,
And cry, "Pox on her, Ned, she can't be sound!"
Then slink away, a fresh one to engage,
With so much seeming heat and loving rage,
You'd frighten listening actress on the stage;
Till she at last has seen you huffing come,
And talk of keeping in the tiring-room,
Yet cannot be provok'd to lead her home.
Next, you Falstaffs of fifty, who beset
Your buckram maidenheads, which your friends get;
And whilst to them you of achievements boast,
They share the booty, and laugh at your cost.
In fine, you essenc'd boys, both old and young,
Who would be thought so eager, brisk, and strong,
Yet do the ladies, not their husbands wrong;
Whose purses for your manhood make excuse,
And keep your Flanders mares for show not use;
Encourag'd by our woman's man to-day,
A Horner's part may vainly think to play;
And may intrigues so bashfully disown,
That they may doubted be by few or none;
May kiss the cards at picquet, ombre, loo,
And so be taught to kiss the lady too;
But, gallants, have a care, faith, what you do.
The world, which to no man his due will give,
You by experience know you can deceive,
And men may still believe you vigorous,
But then we women—there's no cozening us.